Last Resort

Last Resort

Keith W. Wander

CROSSWAY BOOKS • WHEATON, ILLINOIS
A DIVISION OF GOOD NEWS PUBLISHERS

Last Resort.

Published by Crossway Books, a division of
Good News Publishers, Wheaton, Illinois 60187.

Cover illustration: David Yorke

Second printing, 1990

Printed in the United States of America

Library of Congress Catalog Card Number 90-80616

ISBN 0-89107-576-3

Library of Congress Cataloging-in-Publication Data

Wander, Keith, 1941-
    Last resort / Keith Wander.
        p.   cm.
    ISBN 0-89107-576-3
    I. Title.
    PS3573.A4768L3   1990
813' .54--dc20

90-80616
CIP

To Jan,
who believed

Trust in the LORD with all thine heart,
and lean not unto thine own understanding.
In all thy ways acknowledge him,
and he shall direct thy paths.
Be not wise in thine own eyes; fear the LORD,
and depart from evil.
It shall be health to thy navel,
and marrow to thy bones.

PROVERBS 3:5-8 (KJV)

PROLOGUE

Cleveland, Ohio
March, 1963

S he sat by the piano as four portable fans whirled unsuccessfully in an attempt to push air through the smoke and steam which engulfed the room. The lights made her white skin and blonde hair appear even more pale, giving her the appearance of a blonde Kabuki actress. Her hair was swept back into a French twist pinned with a rhinestone barrette which sparkled when she turned her head to look at the piano player. The plunging white dress she wore gave her the appearance of looking cool and unbothered by the heat and noise, but she was betrayed by an occasional bead of perspiration which trickled down from the nape of her neck, across her collarbone, and into her dress.

The piano player frequently looked at her and smiled. Then he would gaze around the room in a slow, easy fashion, catch the eye of a customer at a nearby table, and make a comment. Occasionally the customer would answer back, but the piano player would always continue to play, ending the patter with a laugh or a chuckle. He nodded to her now, and she walked to the edge of the stage with a hand microphone.

Most of the patrons continued to talk and drink. In the back of the room three college students at a small round table nursed their beers and told each other jokes they had told each other before. As the singer began her song, the tallest of the three stopped listening to his two friends. She sang "Fly Me to the

Moon" and searched for someone who seemed to care that she was alive. The tallest student stared at her, enchanted by the sound of her voice and the white-blondness of her body seen through a cone of spotlighted smoke. She swept past him slowly with her eyes, then returned his stare through,

> *"Let me see what life is like*
> *on Jupiter and Mars."*

She closed her eyes through,

> *"In other words, hold my hand.*
> *In other words, darling, kiss me."*

Her eyes opened again with,

> *"Fill my life with song,*
> *and let me sing forevermore.*
> *You are all I long for,*
> *all I worship and adore."*

Her eyes closed during,

> *"In other words,*
> *please be true."*

With a hard stare directly at him she sang,

> *"In other words,*
> *I love you."*

He was the only person in the room who clapped, but he stopped when people at nearby tables looked his way. His two friends laughed, and he wasn't sure if they were laughing at an old joke or him.

"Hudson," said the second student, "do you get it?"

"Get what?" he asked, still staring at the singer.

"Don'tcha get it? The salesman said he hoped he never got that hungry. Don'tcha get it? The rooster and the chickens!"

"Oh yeah, yeah," Hudson answered lamely. "That's a good one."

"A real side-splitter. I can tell by your reaction," teased the third.

She was into the second stanza of "You Made Me Love You" with a solid eye-lock on him. The tempo was upbeat, and she smiled seductively as she sang, "I didn't want to do it, I didn't want to do it." The noise in the room elevated as if the crowd wanted to compete with the music. More drinks, more noise. The second-show crowd paid even less attention than the first-show group. He wanted to jump up and shout at everyone to be quiet so they could hear her. More accurately, he wanted them to be quiet so he could hear her. But he sat still because he was afraid that any movement on his part would disturb the eye contact between them.

During "My Funny Valentine" his two friends ran out of jokes and noticed what was taking place. The singer was alternating between hard stares and closed eyes again. Each time she reopened her eyes she looked only at Hudson. The other two leaned his way and stage-whispered their thoughts.

"Hudson, I think she's in love with you."

"Tell her to look five degrees to the left so she can see the greatest lover in history right before her eyes."

"I've got it—she's a relative of yours and this is a joke."

"Has she seen you naked in the shower or something? No . . . if she had she'd be laughing, not singing."

All through their banter he never stopped staring. She finished the song, and a dozen people clapped politely. She bowed slightly from the waist, which caused his two friends to applaud very loudly. The one on Hudson's left stopped clapping long enough to put his fingers under his tongue and whistle.

When she stood erect she was no longer staring at Hudson. Instead she looked across the room and smiled at those who were applauding, including his two friends. She turned toward the back of the stage, tripped slightly, caught her balance, and exited through a black curtain. The piano player watched her go, played a few chords, then accompanied himself as he sang "Angel Eyes" by Matt Dennis. Few people in the crowd that night knew that the piano player was in fact Matt Dennis himself. Fewer cared.

"My old heart ain't gainin' no ground, while my angel eyes ain't here," he crooned.

"Buy a girl a drink?" asked a black-haired woman with green eye shadow which looked as if it had been applied with a trowel. Pouting her lips like Brigitte Bardot, she slid into the booth next to one of the college boys, then placed her hand on him as she looked longingly into his eyes.

"Baby, you keep that up and I'll buy you this whole lounge," said student three.

Without a signal a waitress was at the table. "Champagne for me," said the B-girl. "A bottle."

"A bottle?" squeaked student three. "How much does a bottle cost?"

"Forty-eight dollars," said the waitress with a bored expression.

"Forty-eight dollars?" he squeaked again. "I don't have that much to last me all semester. How much is a glass?"

"Forty-eight dollars," answered the waitress. "Once we open the bottle it's all the same price."

"How about a beer?" he said to the B-girl hopefully. She stopped rubbing his thigh.

"Beer? What do you think I am?" she fired back indignantly.

"Look, boys," interrupted the waitress, "there's a cover and a minimum here. You've each had two beers all night, which won't make the minimum. We know you snuck into the men's room during the break to avoid the cover charge. If you leave now, we'll forget everything. Otherwise Hector over there may get involved." As she said this she nodded toward a huge man-gorilla in a tuxedo standing by the exit with his arms crossed.

"We're hoping to hear the singer some more," said Hudson.

"Miss Laurie?" snickered the B-girl. "She's gone for the evening."

"What's her name?" asked Hudson.

"Gloria Laurie. She has two first names," said the B- girl. "Trust me, she's done for the night."

"Is that right?" Hudson asked the waitress, who nodded affirmatively.

"Come on, guys," said the second student, "let's go." Then he added in a false macho tone, "We've been thrown out of better places than this." This was a lie, as it was the best place they had been thrown out of. It was, in fact, the only place they had been thrown out of. The student hangouts which they frequented never threw out anyone, which was a tribute to their patience and lack of taste.

"Does this mean the wedding's off?" student three asked the B-girl.

"Kiss off, punk!" she spat.

"But Mother has the caterers and the band all arranged."

The waitress nodded toward Hector. Hudson and student two took their mouthy friend by each arm and led him toward the exit. Over his shoulder he shouted, "What will we tell our friends? What will we do with all the champagne?" He laughed as they reached the exit three steps ahead of Hector.

Matt Dennis finished "Angel Eyes" with

> "My old heart ain't gainin' no ground,
>   while my angel eyes ain't here.
> 'scuse me while I disappear."

The next day a dozen roses arrived at the back door of the lounge for Gloria Laurie. The card attached to the box read, "I enjoyed your show last night. I'll be calling soon. Matt is right. My old heart ain't gainin' no ground while my angel eyes ain't here." It was signed by H. J. Hudson. The janitor put the flowers in her dressing room beside a phone which rang and rang for the next two days. The lounge was closed on Sundays and Mondays, but Hudson didn't know that and continued to call hourly.

On Tuesday afternoon a stagehand answered the phone only to inform him that Gloria Laurie was no longer working at the club but had moved on to Chicago. The stagehand didn't know where in Chicago or at which club she might be working. It was a lie, but it stopped the dumb phone from ringing and allowed the stagehand to get back to his crossword puzzle. After hanging up the phone, the stagehand threw the roses into a garbage can.

ONE

"Ladies and gentlemen, this is your captain speaking. We'll be landing in just a few minutes at Westport International Airport. We hope you've despised the flight on Puddlejump Airlines. Those of us in the crew hated having you aboard. As we approach our landing, the cabin attendants will pass out barf bags to commemorate your trip with us. We hope you'll take them home and put them in a prominent place. If you ever get a chance to fly with us again, please avoid it if at all possible. Have a nice day."

The bus driver looked in the rearview mirror at the crazy kid who was talking to himself. The driver wondered if the kid was on drugs or was drunk. It seemed too early in the day to be drinking, but the driver couldn't figure the kid out. He seemed like an all-right boy when he got on—tall, dressed in khakis and a T-shirt, even had short hair. But he'd been talking out loud to himself for the last thirty miles.

Crazy kid thinks this bus is an airplane, thought the driver to himself. *If he gives me any trouble I'll just reach beneath this seat and smack him with this billy club.* The driver fingered a sawed-off Louisville Slugger which he kept handy for just such occasions.

"Please make sure your seat belts are fastened. The captain has turned on the 'no smoking sign,' so stuff 'em if you've got 'em. Weather today is sunny and dry. The local time in Westport is approximately twenty years behind the rest of civilization." The kid was looking out the window of the bus as he spoke to no one but himself.

The bus's brakes exhaled a gush of air as it pulled in front of the general store. The driver threw the door open and glanced back at his passenger, who continued to talk to himself out loud. "Ladies and gentlemen, please remain seated until the captain has turned off the seat belt sign. If you are traveling to further points with us, please stay on board as our stop will be brief. If you're making connections with another airline, lots of luck because we're the only airline who lands here."

The bus driver had the large cargo door on the side of the bus opened and began unloading cardboard boxes onto a four-wheel cart. He didn't know how he would handle the crazy kid, but he took his duffel bag out of the cargo hold and set it on the sidewalk. The kid got up, walked toward the front of the bus, stepped down the stairs, stretched and yawned. He walked directly at the driver, who suddenly remembered that his Louisville Slugger was still on the bus. The kid stood at attention in front of the driver, snapped his heels together, saluted, and said, "Great landing, captain."

"You all right, son?" the driver asked.

"Sure. You know how it is at these busy terminals. The plane gets in on time, but then they lose your luggage. Why, goodness me, here it comes now." With this he swooped down on his duffel bag and flipped it in a wide arc so that it landed on his left shoulder. He turned around quickly and returned to the driver. "One more thing, captain . . ."

"Yes?" said the driver, totally convinced that he was dealing with a true loony.

"The stewardesses provided poor service."

"We don't have no stewardesses, son."

"It doesn't get much worse than that, does it?" said the kid as he turned and paced off in a long-legged gait.

The manager of the general store came out to greet the driver and sort the packages on the cart. "These all you had on this load, Howard?" he asked.

"Just that and one screwball kid," he said as he nodded in the direction of his passenger.

The store manager squinted and said, "That looks like the Hudson boy. He and his folks come up here every summer. Nothing wrong with him, Howard."

"Oh yeah? Well, he told me our stewardesses provided poor service."

"A little criticism never hurt anyone, Howard." They looked at each other momentarily, then laughed.

The kid walked for a mile, stopping every fifty yards to shift the duffel bag from one shoulder to the other. He had forgotten to eat that day, and in addition to sore arms and shoulders his head was beginning to ache. He was beyond the village limits with no restaurants in sight and only miles of gravel road ahead of him when a large blue 1956 Buick pulled alongside of him. A tiny, white-haired lady who drove by pointing her chin in the air so she could see over the steering wheel rolled down the driver's window cautiously as she slowed the Buick to a stop. "John? John R., is that you?" she asked hesitantly.

"Mrs. Berger . . . Hi," he answered. "Yes, it's me."

She fired questions at him without taking a breath or waiting for an answer to any of her inquiries. "Are your folks up here yet? I haven't seen them. Are they coming to get you? Do you want a ride? You've grown some more, haven't you?"

"Two nos, two yeses, and an order of fries to go," he answered.

"What?"

"I'd like a ride, Mrs. Berger. Thanks." He tossed his duffel bag in the backseat. Mrs. Berger drove slowly, her nose, chin, and eyes peeking over the top of the steering wheel as if she expected to see an alien invader on the other side of the windshield.

"I didn't know your folks were up here already," she said.

"They're not. Only me. I'm here to . . . uh . . . I'm . . . uh . . . I'm going to open it up for them."

"That's nice of you. You out of Michigan State so soon? It's early. What are you studying?"

"Nothing," he said and smiled, hoping she'd get the joke. But her eyes were riveted on the gravel road which was passing by at twenty miles per hour.

"That's nice. State's a good school for that. How's your sister?"

"She's going to have a baby pretty soon."

Mrs. Berger stomped on the brakes, bringing the big Buick to a gravel-crunching halt. "A baby? That's wonderful! I'll bet your folks are excited, aren't they?" Without waiting for his answer she continued, "How long has she been married?" as the Buick began rolling again.

"Almost two years now. She married a doctor at the hospital where she used to work."

"A doctor!" The brakes slammed again. "That's wonderful too. Isn't life full of surprises?"

She pointed the car down the street where the Hudson summer home was located. John R. barely recognized it as tree stumps, roots, and mud clumps lined the sides of the road where white birches, poplars, and pines had once stood. Spring rains had washed mud across the gravel road, forcing Mrs. Berger to gently guide the Buick around potholes filled with brown, brackish water.

"What happened to the street?" he asked in amazement.

"Oh, the dumb village decided to pave it, so they cut down all the trees last winter."

"Doesn't look paved to me. It's ugly."

"They won't pave it either. Village Council says they ran out of money cutting down the trees. Now they don't have enough money to pave the street."

"When do they . . ."

"Oh, in a year, maybe two. Village Council hates to rush things. In the meantime it looks awful, and property values are suffering too. I'll bet your folks will be disappointed, what with your place up for sale."

"For sale? Our place isn't for sale." Mrs. Berger slammed on the brakes, skidding the car to a stop at a real estate sign on the edge of the Hudson property line.

"Isn't life full of surprises?" she asked as John R. stared in disbelief at the *FOR SALE* sign.

"Ladies and gentlemen, the captain has turned on the 'no smoking' sign . . ." The stewardess began her chant without any enthusiasm.

Hudson wondered how many times he had heard that speech in the past five years. It had to be over five hundred, maybe even seven hundred. Mary Alice made his flight arrangements, she'd know. But Mary Alice had quit two weeks ago. He knew he'd miss her.

". . . on behalf of the crew and myself, we want to thank you for flying with us . . ." This time it was the captain.

At least he didn't say, "Have a nice day," thought Hudson as he struggled down the aisle with a briefcase and a two-suit overnighter.

The stewardess stood at the edge of the ramp looking bored. "Have a nice day," she said mechanically.

Hudson snickered to himself. *She needs my book, and she needs to attend one of my seminars*, he thought. *And I need a rental car.* He hoped Mary Alice had taken care of the reservations before she left. He checked his travel packet—there was no reservation slip for a car. *Maybe I didn't tell her, but she always anticipated my needs before*, he argued with himself. *A car will be there. I can visualize it*, he reasoned as he approached the counter.

"Do you have a reservation for a Hudson?" he asked an effeminate-looking young man.

"Oh nooo! They haven't made those in years!" he cackled as he put a limp-wristed hand across his mouth to cover the laughter.

"Good one," lied Hudson, who had heard the same line hundreds of times from rental car clerks.

"Let me see," said the clerk, dancing along a tray of reservation envelopes in Post-Office-sized bins. "Nope, no reservation.

Sorry. But we do have three new Corsicas available if you'd like
a car. It's not the tourist season yet, so we've got extras."

"Great," said Hudson taking out his driver's license and a
credit card. He signed the forms thrown in front of him by the
clerk and pushed them back across the counter.

"There is one problem though," said the clerk with one finger
pointing in the air.

"Yes?"

"Your driver's license has expired. Tut, tut, tut!"

"That's no problem, is it?"

"If you want a car it is!" The clerk raised his eyebrows and
looked shocked.

Hudson argued with him for several minutes without success.
The clerk pointed him toward a bus station with a crooked finger
and wrist that reminded Hudson of the wicked witch in Snow
White. Hudson caught a cab to the bus station and hoped he
hadn't missed the last bus of the day—he didn't have enough cash
to cover cab fare for a sixty-mile ride to his summer home. *Why
don't cabs take credit cards*, he wondered.

The bus station was empty except for a clerk behind iron bars
and a bus driver who was leaning against the counter talking to
her. "Might as well take that ticket from you now," the bus driver
said to him. "Looks like it's just you and me and some cardboard
boxes on this trip."

"I won't complain if you won't," said Hudson as he boarded
the bus.

"Suits me. Anyway, the stewardesses provide poor service."

"How's that again?" asked Hudson as he sank into a seat
behind the driver.

"Nothing," answered the driver. "Just a little bus humor. Next
stop Westport, Michigan. Be ready to set your watch back twenty
years." The driver chuckled to himself for being so witty.

The bus arrived at Westport just as the general store was closing. The other businesses in the village were already closed,

except for Humphrey's Bar and Grill which was open every day until 2 A.M. except on national holidays, Christmas, and Thanksgiving. Many of the local workmen ate and drank at Humphrey's. The tourists preferred the Boar's Head across the street, which was open between Memorial Day and Labor Day. Owned and operated by a gay male nurse, the locals at Humphrey's called that other restaurant the Whore's Head.

Hudson didn't feel comfortable going into Humphrey's with a suit, briefcase, and overnighter to ask someone for a ride home. He had only been to Humphrey's twice. The first time patrons were hanging freshly-shot deer on a large scale outside the bar, and the second time a fight erupted resulting in one drunk patron returning with a chain saw to finish off his adversary as well as the front one-third of Humphrey's bar.

The walk, thought Hudson, *will do me good*. He was thirty pounds overweight as a result of five years of speaking engagements at clubs, conventions, and civic groups. In that period of time he figured he had eaten two herds' worth of prime rib and Swiss steak plus thirty flocks' worth of chicken cooked every way imaginable. His poor eating habits were coupled by an exercise program that consisted of sprinting from one plane to another. He could barely walk up two fights of stairs without getting winded, while ten years ago he was able to play half-court basketball with the high school team without any strain.

He got into a fast-paced rhythm through the first mile and even thought of jogging, but rejected the idea because of his briefcase, overnighter, and wing-tip shoes. He felt invigorated by the cool spring air. In the village he passed houses where women were cooking supper as their husbands read newspapers in overstuffed chairs after long hours in sawmills, repair shops, or farm fields. Hudson loved the beauty in this part of the state. He told people that God tripped one day and when He put His hand down to catch His balance, the lakes, valleys, and natural wonders in the area were formed.

Beyond the village he reached the gravel roads which would take him to his summer home. The house was a product of his thoughts and ideas made three-dimensional through the craft and patience of a skilled builder in the area who tolerated Hudson's many changes as the house progressed. The frame of the house was constructed from barn beams. In addition to providing structural support, the beams became an integral part of the house's decor; both the vertical and horizontal beams were made visible throughout the house. The rough-hewn wood was made less overtly masculine by white walls and pastel paintings which his wife, Jane, had selected. The crowning touch, however, was the bay. The east side of the house was heavily glassed so the beauty of the bay could fill the house. Colors of the water changed from green to blue to black, orange, or a pink-tinged violet depending upon the sky above it. The reflected glory of the bay filled the lower level of the house with hues and shades which never failed to impress Hudson. He hated the idea of selling the house, but knew of no alternative given his current circumstances.

As he reached the final mile, the sun's light began to fade quickly. The birch, pines, and poplars which once stood guard on the gravel lane to his house were lying in random patterns by the roadside like soldiers killed on a field of battle. Some trees had been cut into firewood sections, others had the limbs cut off, but most were left lying where they had been felled by a ravaging chain saw. For the first hundred yards Hudson hoped the damage was localized to accommodate power lines. Instead, he found both sides of the road had been devastated all the way to his house, which was the last one on the road. His disgust was amplified as he walked through rain-filled puddles which soaked his shoes and socks. The gravel road was coated with mud from mounds of dirt which were created as large falling trees tore smaller ones out by the roots.

He reached the house with wing tips which looked as if they were covered with toe rubbers made of mud. The back of his trousers were splattered with brown spots, his feet were soaked, and his arms were sore from the weight of the briefcase and overnighter.

The real estate sign had been pulled out of the lawn, and he fell on all fours as he tripped over it, so that muddy water splashed on his face when his palms hit the ground. Picking himself up he saw a light go on in the den. The shadow of a person crossed the room.

He cursed beneath his breath as he wondered if the intruder was the same vandal who had cut down the trees and ripped out the real estate sign. He hid behind a tree, trying to devise a plan which would scare the intruder from the house. There was a hatchet and an axe in the toolshed, but he didn't want to appear violent if it was a couple of local kids using the place as a love nest. What if, he thought, the drunk who tried to chain saw Humphrey's was in there cutting down his beautiful barn beams? He listened intently. Instead of a chain saw he heard the sounds of a jazz tape which included a version of "Angel Eyes" being played on his stereo. *It is kids*, he thought. *They're using my house, my stereo, and my tapes.* His twelve years as a teacher and coach had taught him that the best approach would be a straight confrontation. No hatchets, no axes, just a frontal attack using fast questions and a loud voice.

He approached the solid oak door and banged it with a mud-covered clenched fist.

TWO

The oak door opened two inches. An eyeball peered at Hudson from the opening between the doorjamb and the door's edge. Three seconds later the door swung open.

"Dad?"

"John R?"

"What are you doing here?" they asked simultaneously, then nervously laughed at their timing. Each felt some tension drain from his body.

"You look good," said Hudson as he put down his mud-coated briefcase and overnighter.

"You look awful. Did you come by car or dune buggy?"

Hudson entered the bathroom and shouted as he washed his hands, "Neither. My driver's license has expired, and I had to take the bus to Westport. I walked home from the general store, but some idiot took the real estate sign out of our front yard and I tripped over it."

"I wonder who would do a dumb thing like that?" said John R. softly.

"What did you say?" asked Hudson, wiping his hands with a towel as he came out of the bathroom.

"I asked where Mom is," John R. responded.

"Well, uh . . . she won't be here . . . For a while that is. She's with your sister until the baby comes, then she'll stay until Carrie can take care of things for herself. Paul has switched hospitals and works all sorts of strange hours. Your mother is worried about Carrie."

"Something wrong with Carrie?"

"No. Your mother has the jitters is all."

"But the baby isn't due for another two months, I thought."

"About two months. But, John R., you know your mother. She worries when she doesn't have anything to worry about."

"I guess. But this sets a new Olympic record even for her. What's with the home being for sale anyway?"

"Oh, I don't know . . . Just getting tired of the upkeep and expense, I guess." Hudson walked into the bedroom to change clothes. John R. followed him.

"Upkeep? You built this place to be almost maintenance-free. I'll help with the upkeep this summer. What do you need done?"

"I'm starved," said Hudson. "Do we have anything here to eat?"

"No," answered John R. "No kidding, Dad, I can do chores around here this summer, and you know I can fix just about anything. What do you need done?"

"Do you think the general store is open yet? No, it was closing when I got off the bus. How about the Boar's Head?"

"Not open yet. What maintenance, Dad? I'll do whatever. I know how you love this place."

Persistence and timing are two key ingredients for success, thought Hudson. *Unfortunately my son has always had them confused.* "O.K., sit down, John R. I didn't want to get into this so soon, but since you insist . . ." They sat across from each other at a circular dining-room table that faced the bay.

"I'm afraid I've lost this house."

"Lost it? How could you lose this house? It's as big as a barn."

"Do you want to hear this or joke around?"

John R.'s eyes darted away from his father.

"It's tough enough without the jokes," said Hudson in a stern voice. "Just listen, O.K.?"

John R. looked back at Hudson and nodded.

"I put this place up as collateral on a business deal that is going belly up."

l

"A Greek restaurant?" Hudson glared at John R. "Sorry. I'll be good, I promise."

Hudson held his temper in check. He thought of exploding at his son as a way of diverting the conversation, but knew that John R. would open the subject again at another time. "It was going to be a car factory . . . Classic cars . . . One line actually . . . Cords . . . Beautiful cars . . . Rounded fenders, front wheel drive, fancy side pipes, leather interiors. We were going to produce replicas of the convertible and the sedan. Each car would have been custom-built with tender love and care."

"We?"

"Two others and me. One guy was a car expert. He retired early from GM and knew how to assemble the car using a GM chassis and frame. The other said he had connections with a parts producer, so that we could get body molds produced out of fiberglass. He knew a parts plant that was hungry for business and would be willing to work with us."

"Sounds good so far."

"That's the good news. I was on the road over 240 days last year. During that time the GM guy's wife developed cancer, so the third partner thought it would be smart to invest our money in the stock market while the doctors determined how serious her problem was. It made sense because the stock market was going up like crazy at the time and we could make money even with the project on hold.

"We invested in futures, which I didn't know much about but sure learned the hard way. Our expert in this area said it was the best way to earn money—making other people's money work as hard as ours. I don't know how other people's money did, but ours worked so hard it got exhausted. Last October when Black Monday struck I knew by early afternoon that we were in trouble. We decided to cut our losses, but couldn't get a phone call through to sell in time because the market was so backed up.

"Despite our bad fortune, the parts producer who was going to supply us with molds landed a big contract with Ford and Chrysler, so we were put on a back burner. The plant we were targeted to buy was bought by a Japanese electronics firm, so we took an option on another place which would eventually cost us twice the price of the first. We started to do some rough calculations, and by the time we figured real estate, tooling costs, payroll, benefits packages, and taxes we were in deep financial trouble. Our original estimate of a moderately priced specialty car had ballooned to more than a new Rolls Royce.

"The GM guy's wife died, and his motivation to take on this headache died also. Our financial genius invested in a few more long shots to try get us even, and they failed even worse than the futures market. I should have listened to Mark Twain's advice instead."

"Mark Twain was in the stock market?" John R. asked.

"Enough to know more than I did about it. He said something like, 'October. This is one of the peculiarly dangerous months to speculate in stocks. Others are November, December, January, February, March, April, May, June, July, August, and September.' At any rate, I've got to sell this place to settle some debts which are staring me in the face."

Most of this was confusing to John R., who said, "But you can come back, can't you? You're giving plenty of talks, and your book is still selling well, isn't it?"

"Right now I'm doing some seminars sponsored by Rotary Clubs, PTA's, and Kiwanis Clubs throughout America, but my fee is down to 55 percent of its original amount. I'm a long way from sharing the platform with Zig Ziglar, Art Linkletter, and Robert Schuller like I did that weekend in Memphis. And my book is given away at the seminars, otherwise it would be out of print. It's just not selling anymore. I should have written another, but I spent too much time on the road to bother. Now here I am, the author of one of the hottest-selling 'how to' books on goal accomplishment and about to lose everything because of a lack of planning."

"Isn't there something we can do?"

"Well, I'm working on another angle. Over Memorial Day weekend I'm having a group of people up here. There will be several investors plus a studio which is thinking about making a videotape and movie series of the book's concepts."

"All right!" exclaimed John R. "Can I play the romantic lead?"

"Not that kind of movie, smart guy. It's for educational purposes. Businesses use these sessions for executive education and training. I did a similar thing live at a Digital Equipment sales seminar in Boston one week. I don't know how you do a video series and keep it interesting, but that's why the studio people will send someone here."

"Sounds good. By Memorial Day I should be able to have my room picked up."

Hudson smiled faintly. "You asked before how you could help, remember?"

John R. nodded.

"There's a ton of things that have to be done around here. Without your mother around, the place hasn't a chance of looking decent with you here alone. I'll leave Mrs. Berger's phone number. She'll get the place looking nice. I'm also hoping to take some of the people out on the boat. You could make sure it gets off the cradle and into the water on time. I've got a list of twenty things that need attention. If we could split them up it would help me out."

"Terrific. I'll have everything ready for you."

"One more task got added to the original list. We'll need to park cars for our guests. What happened to our street anyway?"

"Mrs. Berger told me the village was going to pave the street, but ran out of money after they cut down the trees."

"Ran out of money? I can relate to that," said Hudson with a twisted grin.

During the next two weeks John R. completed all the tasks his father had assigned him plus others which he initiated on his own. He cleared the beach of wild grass and removed the dead wood which had been washed into the bay by the spring rains. He supervised the floating of their boat, then swept and polished it with painstaking care. He oiled the teak and buffed the stainless steel to a glistening shine.

John R. took a special pride in the family's boat because Hudson had taken him to all the boat dealers when they decided to purchase the "boat of their dreams." Hudson and John R. discussed the features of every model even though he was only twelve years old at the time. Hudson listened to his son's observations with genuine interest, which was a wise thing to do since Hudson knew little about anything mechanical whereas John R. had demonstrated a surprisingly gifted mechanical aptitude through his ability to repair household appliances, a skill which astounded Hudson.

For John R., mechanical devices had a logic that was clear and understandable, which was more than he could say about his knowledge of girls, including his sister. Girls giggled and screamed a lot. They also whispered and giggled some more. And whispered and giggled and screamed, then cried. He never understood how they found so much to giggle, whisper, scream, or cry about. John R. preferred fixing his mother's broken vacuum cleaner to talking to a girl any day. At least you knew when the vacuum cleaner was broken and when it wasn't.

When the choice of boats had been narrowed down to two makes, Hudson decided it would be smart for the two of them to visit the plants where the boats would be made. While Hudson was willing to toss a coin in the air as a way of making his decision, John R. pointed out the easier access to the twin Crusader engines on the thirty-six-foot Tiara, which became their final choice. What Hudson didn't know was that John R. made his selection based on the fact that the dealer and factory were willing to customize the cockpit area so there would be additional lounge space topside. This would allow John R. to sit on one side of the boat with his friends while Carrie and her friends could sit on the other side to whisper, giggle, scream, and cry to their hearts' content. At least he wouldn't have to sit next to them while they carried on.

The boat was used for business purposes by Hudson during the time he was selling insurance, and a special touch was needed to close a large life insurance deal. A trip on the boat seemed to convince prospective clients that their agent was someone who took a personal interest in them, a friend who wanted to spend time with them rather than simply sell them a big insurance policy. They were wrong. Jane teased Hudson that a portion of his commissions should go to John R. for his selection of the boat.

Jane was the one member of the family who originally opposed the purchase of the Tiara. For her, it was an enormous outlay of money, costing more than the average person's home. She had never been able to shed the memories of childhood when her father and mother bought day-old bread because it was five cents a loaf cheaper. They had lived through the Depression and instilled in her the fear that such a time could return suddenly and without warning. The purchase of a boat of any kind would have sent shivers up and down her parents' spines. But this was not just any boat. This was a beautiful, white, roomy boat complete with a galley, standing head, two berths, and a gas tank which held over three hundred gallons of fuel. While Jane eventually changed her mind about owning the the the boat, she never could get accustomed to filling the tank, which resulted in the payment of nearly four hundred dollars to the marina attendant.

And there was the business of naming the boat. Hudson had been fascinated with a song called "Angel Eyes" for the past several years. He found a jazz and ballad version of the song on one of his many business trips and for some reason insisted on naming the boat after that song. It didn't make much sense to her, but then, owning a thirty-six-foot boat which could be used only four months each year didn't make much sense to her either.

What Jane did enjoy about boating was that it was the one activity in which the family was forced to sit and talk to one another for at least an hour at a time without any interruptions. Over the objections of John R. and Carrie, Jane insisted that a television would not be brought onto the boat. Over Hudson's objections she remained firm that no portable or cellular phone would be placed aboard either. Jane never knew (and Hudson never told her) that one was available through the ship-to-shore radio, and he was careful never to use it when she was aboard.

While the kids swam off the platform on the stern, Jane and Hudson talked about their hopes for each of the children. John R. was growing tall too quickly, worried Hudson. While John R. would copy his father's height, he had none of Hudson's quick reflexes or coordination which had made him a basketball star in high school and college. As a high school coach, Hudson took John R. to practices with him and was forced to face the fact that his son had little natural ability and would only be able to participate in athletics through extra hours of practice. Hudson was willing to spend the extra practice time with John R. as he dreamed of coaching his son on a high school championship team, but John R. just didn't have what it takes. By contrast, Carrie was well-coordinated and a gifted athlete. But to her father's dismay she had no interest in competitive sports. Outgoing and personable, she captained the cheerleading squad as a junior and senior in high school, which was the closest she came to an athletic field. Despite her father's urgings Carrie showed no interest in girls' basketball, volleyball, track, or swimming. Hudson was never able to give a clear answer to people when they asked why neither of his children were involved in sports. John R. was able to answer the question quite bluntly. He said, "Because I'm lousy and she's a dip."

Jane enjoyed day-trips on the boat best of all. She would pack a lunch, and after several hours in the sun they would go below deck to eat. When there was no specific destination in mind, each person knew the day would be devoted to laughing, teasing, and listening. While John R. and Carrie complained that such trips were getting boring, they preferred them to the longer ventures which excited Hudson's competitive spirit, forcing them into big waves and dangerous waters in an effort to reach a specific destination in a minimal amount of time. Jane said Hudson even turned getting to work into competition. He denied this, but knew that there were three ways to get to his office and one was two minutes and ten seconds faster than the others.

John R. took a special interest in maintaining the boat. He fired the engines to keep the batteries charged, checked the gauges for any obvious mechanical difficulties, and even became adept at tuning the engines by himself. Hudson was both pleased and amazed at his son's abilities to spot potential problems. At one point the hoses to the bilge blower had been disconnected, and the possibility for an explosion in the engine compartment was averted by John R.'s keen eye.

Working on boats never seemed like work to John R. He was fascinated by them. Spare moments were spent walking up and down slip spaces to identify the characteristics of each boat tied there. While others his age knew the makes and models of domestic and foreign cars, John R. knew the makes and models of power and sailboats. They had been coming to northern Michigan for three summers, and during the second summer John R. became so well-known around the marina that he was hired as a marina attendant whose duties involved pumping gas, directing transient boaters to open slip spaces, and light maintenance.

Now, two days before his father had to get back to his work, John R. received a letter notifying him he was rehired for the summer of '88 as a marina attendant. He was elated. The next day he received a letter from his mother which had the opposite effect on him.

THREE

Dear John R.,

Nice going, pal. First you have a telephone message created, then you program your roommate to lie for you, and before long the whole world will believe you're still in college. Not your mother. What did Mr. Rogers say about fooling some of the people some of the time but you can't fool Mom? Or was that Captain Kangaroo? So how long have you been out of school? Here I was all worried that you wouldn't find anyone home when you got there, that you wouldn't have anything to eat. I individually wrapped twenty-four lasagna dinners and twelve chicken breasts and put them in the freezer for you. What am I supposed to do with them now? I suppose this means you're going to live on a balanced diet of pizza, hamburger, and peanut butter. If you die this summer and they do an autopsy on you and say he must have had a lousy mother because his veins were loaded with cholesterol, I swear I'll never speak to you again.

Now to other matters . . . I understand your father told you I wouldn't be with you this summer. He told me you were going to help him out. That's nice. He also chickened out from telling you the real story. Why is it that your father can give speeches to thousands of people and not get nervous, yet he turns into a coward when it comes to telling his family anything important? I will be staying with Carrie this summer, as Paul is working all kinds of hours and has National Guard camp to attend. However, that's not the real reason I'll be there.

What your father told you about our financial situation is true. We are in deep yogurt this time. My mother and father were right all along. They must be smiling in their graves saying, "I told you, I told you, but would you listen?" Even Mary Alice quit as his secretary because he was behind on the payroll and she knew there wasn't a secure future working for him. But money or the lack of it isn't that big an issue for me. When we started out and your father was coaching, we lived in little tacky rented houses and drove old cars held together by scotch tape and baling wire. In many ways I miss the excitement of those days. Whatever our money problems are, we can work around them.

I've gone through a series of mood swings on this whole situation. I've been shocked, angry, hurt, but mainly guilty. I'm sure that if I had done some things differently it would have all worked out. There had to be ways in which I behaved that caused him to act this way. I'm going to talk to Carrie about it while I'm with her. Women have a way of being brutally frank with each other.

Right now I seem to be stuck in an angry cycle. I'm mad at him, I'm mad at you for not telling me you dropped out of school, and I'm mad at myself for being mad at both of you. I'll be driving to your sister's, so don't try to call. I'm going to stop and visit friends and relatives along the way. Right now a slow drive to California is the best therapy for me. I can listen to whatever radio station I want, and I don't have to argue with you.

Take good care of yourself this summer, buddy. Help your dad out all you can. When I call I don't want to hear any wisecracks about my getting old since I'll be a grandmother. I was seventeen once, and I thought grandparents were old and wise. Now I'm forty-seven, about to be a grandmother, and find that grandparents are neither old nor wise. They are merely older and wiser than some seventeen-year-olds, which in certain cases isn't saying much.

Love,
Mom

FOUR

He was wearing the uniform of a marina attendant—tan pants, red polo shirt, and a plastic name tag with *JOHN R.* printed in block letters. *Westport* was stitched on the band of each shirt sleeve in white script. Lying on a webbed chaise lounge on the rear porch, he heard one car door slam, then another. A muffled man's voice followed by a woman's brought a smile to his face as he swung his legs off the lounge, flicked his hair, and splashed cold water on his face.

The trunk of the car was open, blocking a view of his father whose laugh John R. recognized. He snuck alongside the car and bent over, hidden from view although he was able to see Hudson unloading suitcases from the trunk. John R. made a fist with each hand and placed them on top of his head like Mickey Mouse ears. He popped up by the rear fender and squeaked in his best mouse voice, "Hi there, hey there, ho there, you're as welcome as can be."

The trunk lid slammed. Hudson and a woman John R. had never seen before stared at him wide-eyed. After several seconds of silence, Hudson said, "This is my son, John. We call him John R. John R., this is Doctor Medoc."

John R. still had his fists on top of his head. "Hi," he said with an embarrassed grin.

"John R.," said Doctor Medoc extending her hand, "how nice to meet you." She squeezed his hand firmly. "And what an unusual welcome."

"Yeah, well I thought . . . say, is somebody sick?" inquired John R.

"Not that I know of," answered Doctor Medoc. "Why do you ask?"

"I thought Dad called you *Doctor* Medoc."

"Oh that," she smiled. "Actually I'm a Ph.D., not a medical doctor. Don't feel badly—many people are confused by the title."

"Why do you use it then?"

"I beg your pardon?" she responded.

"If you know it confuses people, why do you call yourself doctor? It doesn't seem like a Ph.D. kind of thing to do."

"John R.," interrupted Hudson, "that is not polite."

"No, it's quite all right," Doctor Medoc corrected. "The boy has a good point. Why don't you just call me Maggie, John R."

"I'd rather call you Miss or Mrs. Medoc."

"I prefer Ms. to Miss or Mrs."

"How about Doctor Ms. Medoc?"

"Call me Maggie," she insisted.

"John R., take Maggie's bags to the guest bedroom," said Hudson giving John R. a head nod to get moving.

"Oh, that won't be necessary, Hudson," she responded. John R. stared at her quizzically. "I must carry my own baggage, as we say in the trade."

"No, please, I'll do it, Doctor—that is, Ms. Medoc—Maggie," said John R. Both he and Maggie had a grip on the suitcase and were bent over staring each other in the eye.

John R. pulled on the suitcase handle, and Maggie came stumbling toward him, but refused to release her grip. She pulled back, and John R.'s long arms extended straight out until he was pulled toward her with two stumbling steps. He refused to let go of the handle. Once again they were staring at each other, foreheads only inches apart, vise-like grips on the handle of the suitcase which was being yanked back and forth like a two-man saw. He yanked again, she pulled back. Yank, pull . . . yank, pull.

"Very well," she said in exasperation, "if it's so important to you, take it. It *is* the macho thing to do."

John R. carried her bags to the guest room as Hudson showed her around the house. While Maggie was upstairs changing clothes, Hudson hustled John R. out onto the rear deck overlooking the bay.

"John R., you and I need to have a talk."

"Great, Dad, let's start with this letter from Mom."

Hudson snapped the letter from his son's hand and read the first paragraph. "You dropped out of college?"

"That's not the important part," said John R.

"What do you mean?" Hudson interrupted. "You drop out of college, create a string of lies to cover yourself, and say it's not important?"

"Yes, it's important, but it's not the most important part of the letter."

"Well, I don't have time for the rest of the letter right now. For the moment I want to tell you about good manners and Maggie—Doctor Medoc. She is very important to me in terms of my newest project. She's been assigned by the video company to convert my book into a tape series. I don't need you lousing it up with any wise-guy antics."

"My manners? I was trying to be polite."

"Well, that whole 'Doctor—Miss—Mrs.—Ms.' routine was uncalled for. And you almost got into a tug-of-war over her suitcase."

"I was trying to help," answered John R. defensively. "Why did she want to carry her dumb luggage anyway? Besides, did you hear how she said 'boy'? I'm seventeen years old and six foot five. Do I look like a boy? If I were black she wouldn't have said that. How old is she anyway?"

"I don't know. Late twenties or early thirties, I'd guess. Look, you've got to realize that Maggie is an assertive woman."

"So when I do something dumb it's bad manners and when she makes a mistake it's because she's assertive?"

"It's not a perfect world, buddy. You've got to learn that."

"Did I hear someone say perfect?" chirped Maggie from the doorway. She had changed from her gray suit and pumps to designer jeans and running shoes. "This view of the bay may not be perfect, Hudson, but it is close. By the way, I couldn't help but admire all the plaques and awards you've won. The wall in the den is covered with them."

"Those are just the ones up here," John R. responded. "He's got a room at home full of trophies."

"I'm impressed!" Maggie gushed. "And how about you, John R.? Do you have awards too?"

"They're all hanging on that wall right there." He pointed to a bare white wall in the great room.

"But that wall is blank."

"It is? For cryin' out loud, I've been ripped off."

Maggie gave him a serious, analytical look. "Don't you enjoy athletics?" she asked.

"I enjoy them O.K., but I was born with a severe congenital disease."

"Oh, I'm so sorry," she said earnestly. "May I ask what it is?"

"Sure . . . I stink."

Hudson interrupted. "John R. has never been willing to put in the extra work needed to be a true competitor. He has talents in other areas, however."

"I do?"

"You skipped the eighth grade and graduated a year ahead of everyone in your class. Of course I had to push you to do it, but you've always needed to be pushed."

"Yeah, well, they don't give out any trophies for skipping the eighth grade," John R. answered.

"You're also very creative. The stories you create may get you a prize someday. And you have a sense of humor which not every-one understands—but you have one nonetheless."

"I think you're quite witty, John R.," Maggie said. "Don't let your old dad tease you too much." As she said "old dad" she grabbed Hudson around the neck as if she were going to strangle him. It was done as a playful gesture, but it was the same one which Jane did to Hudson frequently, and it disturbed John R. to see this stranger act in a way similar to his mother.

"Just what is it you do for this video company . . . Maggie?" John R. added her name almost as an afterthought.

"I will teach your father how to write performance-based objectives so his book can be filmed in segments that deliver competency-based training modules," she answered.

"Dad, if I've told you once I've told you a hundred times that was the trouble with your book. It didn't have any of that stuff in it. No cartoons either."

"What does that translate into in layman's English?" Hudson asked Maggie seriously.

"Simply," she began, "your book is a typical how-to book full of attitudinal mumbo jumbo that doesn't wash. What we need to do is convert it into behaviors, visible demonstrations that more clearly define the concepts. We hope to take the ideology you've espoused and make it more visual, more external rather than internal."

"Before we label things too quickly, Dr. Medoc," Hudson answered heatedly, "I must remind you that my 'mumbo jumbo' as you put it has over 350,000 copies in print and was a big part of how those plaques you admired were won. I used the attitudinal approach which you say doesn't wash."

"But, Hudson, it doesn't always translate from one medium to another. You're going to have be a little less defensive." She began to massage the back of his neck.

"I just thought you took a cheap shot," Hudson murmured.

"Dad, Maggie is just an assertive woman."

"Why, thank you, John R.," Maggie replied enthusiastically. "That is a very keen observation on your part, and I appreciate it."

"No problem," said John R. as he left the room. He mumbled to himself, "I wonder if I barfed right now, would it be considered bad manners or assertive?"

"Where are you going?" called Hudson as Maggie was massaging his shoulders.

"I've got to work the third shift at the marina tonight," yelled John R. from the front door.

"Since when does the marina have a third shift?" Hudson yelled back.

"Just started this year." John R. closed the door and began walking. He stopped, turned back toward the house, and said, "Of course I just lied. But then, it's not a perfect world. You've got to learn that, Dad."

John R. "worked" the third shift that night and the one following that: he slept aboard the family boat, *Angel Eyes*. At the end of the second night he decided to return home before dawn and sneak into his bed to give the impression he had come home late the previous evening. He invented a story about being offered a ride home by another attendant whose car broke down, forcing the driver to go for help while John R. stayed with the car to guard the new stereo system. His parents believed anything as long as he used the words stereo, music, or records in a sentence.

The only thing he couldn't do was listen to a stereo, music, or records while they were around. "What's that racket you're playing?" "A stereo." "Turn it off!" Or, "I suppose you call that noise music?" "Yes. It's U-2's newest record." "Turn it off!"

The door opened noiselessly as he entered the foyer. He slipped out of his deck shoes, bare feet slapping softly on the hardwood floor. He had not eaten the night before, so he decided to make a peanut butter sandwich before sneaking up to his room. He tiptoed around the kitchen hunched over at the waist as if a low silhouette would make him quieter as well as less visible. As he ate the sandwich he stood upright, then bent over to reach for a can of Pepsi from the refrigerator, the half-eaten sandwich stuck in his mouth. He bent over again as he placed one hand above the pop tab to muffle the sound as he snapped open the can. He popped up and down, bowing at the waist as he danced to a rock tune which he quietly hummed to himself, now and then softly singing a line from the song.

Meanwhile, Maggie was standing on the deck looking out onto the bay. Wearing an oversized man's shirt as a nightgown, she cradled a cup of coffee in both hands to keep them warm. As the sun began to rise, the light shone through the shirt, which was the only clothing she wore except for a pair of fluffy yellow slippers. She was unaware of John R. moving around the kitchen looking like a giant rooster pecking at a peanut butter sandwich. He was unaware of her too until he popped the tab on the Pepsi.

She gasped audibly and spun back toward the house. As she moved, John R. was conscious of another's presence, and his eyes widened with a fear that he had been caught by his father. He was momentarily relieved to see it was Maggie, until he saw that she was naked beneath the shirt. He stared at her, a peanut butter sandwich in his mouth, eyes wide open, and both hands wrapped around the Pepsi can as it fizzed soda onto the kitchen floor. She stared back at him, both hands still wrapped around a coffee cup which provided less heat than the rush of adrenaline pumping through her body. Separated by twenty feet and a glass sliding door, they stood frozen, unsure what to do next.

Maggie slid the door open after several more seconds of the stare-down. John R. stood motionless, half a peanut butter sandwich in his mouth, both hands clutching the Pepsi can as if he were protecting it from being ripped out of his hands. His eyes were wider than when he first saw her.

Her slippers scuffed in tiny shuffle steps as she walked toward him holding the bottom of the shirt. On the shirt's pocket was the stitched blue monogram HJH. Henry John Hudson. An embarrassed grin crossed her face. "I'd put a coin in the can if I had one, but as you can see, I forgot my purse." She pointed at his sandwich and added, "By the way, I think your harmonica is broken."

He heard the scuff of her yellow slippers against the hardwood floor, but didn't move until he heard a bedroom door close.

Within half an hour John R. stuffed his clothes into his duffel bag and headed back to *Angel Eyes*. His mother's letter was becoming clearer to him. He was angry with his father, although the anger didn't come as easily as it did toward Maggie. The rage he felt toward her came out in a flurry of punches into the duffel bag. He pummeled the bag until his arms became sore and his forehead dripped with perspiration. "How do you like those competencies, you stuffed shirt?" he said to the duffel bag, then kicked it.

Physically drained, he flopped onto the bed and plotted ways to humiliate her, to gain revenge. He surprised himself with the numerous brutal schemes he invented to destroy her. Vicious ideas clashed with each other, but he hoped for a more public humiliation, a scheme which would ridicule her fancy talk, her "assertiveness," her hold on his father. The hate he felt toward her came to him, but ways to get back at her were a scrambled mixture of violence and bizarre behaviors such as labeling all her clothes with a giant letter *A* made out of peanut butter. Physically and mentally exhausted, he fell into a fitful sleep, frustrated that he had no clear plan about the exact technique he would use to gain revenge.

FIVE

The boat rocked. Footsteps overhead woke John R., and he bounded up the steps to find his father sitting in the captain's chair.

"Good morning," said Hudson too cheerily. "I didn't mean to wake you, but I thought I'd check her out before I left. How's she running?"

"I don't know. O.K., I guess. I start her up to keep the batteries charged, check the gauges. Seems to be fine."

Hudson adjusted the throttles, turned the ignition, and fired the engines. They sounded like an operatic baritone humming scales as he increased and decreased the RPMs. In idle they emitted a deep, rumbling sound, inviting the driver to test their power.

"Let's take her out for a run, John R."

"No . . . that's O.K., I've got things to do."

"Come on, it's a beautiful day. Bright sun, light wind, no chop. We'll do like we used to do when you were a kid. We'll run around for a while, then turn her off and float, talk, and get a tan. It'll be just like old times."

It will never be like old times again, thought John R., but contained himself. "Can't do it, Dad. Got too much to do."

"Just for an hour or so. I'm leaving soon. I thought we could spend some time together . . . Just you and me."

Maggie must get seasick, thought John R., but again refrained from saying so. He was struck with another thought. "I'll go with you under one condition: we'll talk about Mom's letter . . . The whole letter, not just the first paragraph."

Hudson thought for several moments before he answered. "All right, I think I can handle it if you can. As a matter of fact, let's stay out there until we understand each other."

"Maybe we should set a more realistic goal, Dad." They looked at each other a few moments, then smiled. John R. scampered across the bow to untie the lines from the cleats. Within minutes they exited the marina and headed for the bay.

The bay was forty miles long from its base to the point where it was fed by Lake Michigan. Protected from winds on the east and west side, numerous peninsulas jutted into it, forming protected coves which made the waters friendlier to smaller boats than those of "the big lake."

One of the peninsulas was Westport Pointe. Those who lived there referred to it simply as The Pointe. From the air The Pointe looked like a large index finger jutting out from a clenched fist. John R. said it was a statement the people on The Pointe were making to the rest of the world. Exclusivity on The Pointe was well-known and not without cost to its residents. The Pointe was protected by its own private police and fire departments, while residents played golf on a club opened only to Pointe landowners. A private airport provided Pointe husbands a runway for their company planes which took them to and from wives and children who stayed throughout the summer. Houses were never sold on The Pointe; they were passed along from generation to generation.

The cove at The Pointe provided the smoothest waters and best fishing, to the dismay of many Pointe residents. Fishermen who had too much to drink or those who experienced engine problems were ill-advised to land along The Pointe's beaches for help. The private police took a twisted pride in making any assault on The Pointe's beachhead an unpleasant experience. One perch fisherman joked that he had been more warmly welcomed

by the Germans at Normandy than he was by the private police
on The Pointe.

Hudson and John R. took turns at the wheel of *Angel Eyes*.
The May sun was not warm enough to overcome the chill produced by the wind brushing the surface of the blue-green
Michigan waters. Within minutes both were shivering, although
neither would admit to being cold. When John R. drove the boat,
he stood straight up, his six foot five frame towering over the
windshield. The chilly air against his face caused his eyes to tear.

Hudson sat in the captain's chair smiling broadly at the Tiara's
performance and the beauty of this northern Michigan coastline.
He viewed the long, white ribbon beaches and occasional houses
within glens of pine trees that looked like little children peeking
out from behind closed doors. Hudson swung the boat in a wide
arc and headed toward the cove at Westport Pointe. Inside the
cove he pulled back to neutral, idled the engines, then shut them
off.

"Should be a good place to anchor, don't you think?"

"Here at The Pointe?" asked John R. "The Coast Guard may
escort us out of Pointe territorial waters if we're seen."

"Pointe people aren't as bad as everyone says. I'll bet you
haven't even seen or talked to any Pointe people all the time
you've been here," chided Hudson as he dropped an anchor.

"I've talked to plenty of them," John R. corrected.

"When? Where?"

"They come into the marina. Though they all have private
slips at their houses, they have to come to us for fuel and to have
their toilets pumped out."

"And what do these mean people say to you when they come
in for service?"

"'Fill her up and pump her out.'"

"And nice people say something different?"

"It's not what they say, Dad—it's how they say it." John R. got
a sneer on his face and growled, "'Fill 'er up and pump 'er out!'"

"Well, I'm not too sure the rest of us outside The Pointe aren't
just a little jealous and make up stories. I happen to know some

of those people too. Did you know that one of them made an anonymous contribution to the hospital fund that was so large the site for the hospital was purchased without the need for a bond issue? And another pays for the planting and maintenance of all the flowers throughout the village. And a third has ice cream cups sent to the county orphans' home daily at his expense. Pretty generous, I'd say, for mean people."

"Do you believe that?"

"Let me give you a line from one of my talks, John R. 'A person is capable of believing only what he can visualize as the truth.' Can I visualize Pointe people being rotten? Sure . . . some. But being rich doesn't make them all villains either. Can I visualize them as being generous? Again, some—not all. I think if you get inside The Pointe you'll find the same cross section of people as the rest of society."

"If I ever get inside The Pointe, I'll let you know. As well-known as you are, they've never invited you out there."

"Oh, I've been invited to play golf a couple of times. I know a few of them, and you'll get to meet them very soon."

"How?"

"The Memorial Day weekend. I'm having a big party at our place to raise some money for the video project. Several Pointe people will be there, and you can gain firsthand experience."

"Oh yeah, the video thing," said John R., not referring to Maggie.

"Yes, we'll talk about that . . . But our deal was to discuss your mother's letter. Can I read it again please?" This time he read the whole letter. There was no expression on his face. He looked up at John R. as if to speak, but reread the letter instead.

"Where would you like me to begin?" he asked his son quietly.

"I don't care . . . Anywhere."

"Well, how about your dropping out of college?"

"I thought we were going to talk about the whole letter," John R. answered angrily.

"We will. That's just where the letter starts," Hudson shot back. He softened the tone of his voice, "Look, if I promise to lis-

ten to you and not lecture, can we start there and then move on
to the other parts? I'll listen, I promise."

"O.K., I guess. But if you break your promise I'm walking
home."

"It wouldn't be a first, but I'd be impressed." Hudson smiled.
"So how long have you been out of school—unofficially that is."

"About halfway through the second semester I stopped going
to classes. I lived in the dorm, got a job at McDonald's, and hung
around campus. You can do that, y' know. Nobody knows if
you're a student or not. Just for the fun of it I made up my own
schedule each day. I looked at the offerings for the spring semester
and went to the classes that sounded interesting. You can do that
too, y' know. Nobody asks what you're doing there. I'd just sit
down, and the professor would start to lecture, and the students
would take notes. At the end of an hour—poof! Everyone disappears. In one semester I took seventy-two different classes.
According to my advisor I needed about forty classes to graduate,
so I declared myself well beyond the minimum requirements and
left."

"I'm sure you're aware that's not how the system works." The
May sun had taken the chill from their bodies, and they took
more comfortable positions at the stern.

"That's the crazy part, Dad. When the system works it's broken, and when it's broken it works."

"How's that?"

"According to my class schedule I had courses in American Lit,
Business Management, Western Civilization, and Psychology.
American Lit was taught by a Pakistani graduate student who I
could barely understand. The first book we read was *Huckleberry Finn*. Do you know how tough it is to comprehend
Huckleberry Finn when it's explained by a Pakistani graduate
student?

"Western Civilization was instructed by a Chinese professor.
Whenever he talked about 'de Lomans' and 'de Gleeks' I thought
he was talking about characters from *Death of a Salesman*.

"My Management course was instructed by a guy at least a

hundred years old who has written three books including our text. The only problem is that he's never managed anybody or anything in his life. My manager at McDonald's has more practical experience than this guy who's an expert.

"And my Psych prof was the real winner. He has a tattoo of numbers on his forearm."

"That was done to Jews during World War Two. The Nazis forced it on them in concentration camps," Hudson chided. "You should be sensitive to the man."

"Yeah? This guy is a twenty-nine-year-old Italian from New Jersey. He said he had gone through an identity crisis in his life, and he had the numbers put on to give his life meaning."

"All of college isn't like that, John R."

"Right, that's what I found out. I invented my own curriculum and dropped in on some classes that were great. I visited some Astronomy classes that were fascinating. I went to two Electrical Engineering labs and I didn't understand a thing, but the teacher was so excited and believed so much in what he was doing that I got excited too. There were some great offerings in Medicine, Pre-law, Music, and Economics. The international monetary situation is in sad shape, y' know. Latin America has us by the throat. When I took everything I was interested in, I declared myself smart enough to work at McDonald's but too young for graduate school. Then I came here for the summer."

"Is that it?"

"Not entirely. College is a strange place, Dad. There's a bunch of students who get drunk every weekend, talk about sex constantly, destroy property, and hire the ACLU to defend their right to do it. Professors are people who can't cure anything but insist on being called doctor. I got to thinking—if this is what higher education is all about, it is way over my head because I don't understand it. Maybe if I dropped out for a year or two, joined the Navy or something, I'd get smart enough to figure out what's missing in my life that advanced education can help with."

"John R., you make up so many stories, I don't know when you're serious and when you're joking around."

"My whole life is a joke." He reflected for a moment, then said, "But that letter in your hand is serious. What gives?"

Hudson's face reddened. He stood up and stared at a large house on The Pointe. He began speaking without looking at his son. "I don't expect you to understand this entirely. For the past several months I've had a vision of what my life would be for the next ten years. The money situation is even worse than your mother's description. When I knew I was in trouble I began to start thinking about starting all over again. I got tired just thinking about it." He sat down heavily and shot a quick glance at John R., although he avoided making eye contact.

"Crazy as it seems, I eventually became energized by starting again, but only after I had constructed a new approach toward life. I began to approach life as if I were a new college graduate. It was exciting—like being twenty-two again. Instead of looking backward with regret, I viewed life as a chance to do all the things I didn't do when I first started out. Most of life would be the same—no money, no security, no prospects for anything promising. But there is so much unfinished business in my life that needs to be completed . . ."

"Unfinished business?"

"Yeah, things I didn't do that I wish I had done or at least tried to do. Some I'll never get a chance to do over again, I know." Hudson lowered his voice as he stroked the smooth teak rail with his fingertips. "I never told my father I loved him. Pretty silly, isn't it?"

He looked up at John R. Hudson's eyes were misty. "Even when he was dying I didn't say anything except lies like he was going to get better and the doctors were going to find a cure for cancer soon."

"I think Grandpa knew, Dad."

"May have, probably did. But it doesn't relieve the agony of knowing I didn't say it." He sighed. "Anyway, I began to think of all the things in my life that needed to be finished. Before long I was getting pumped up. I've got some money protected from the legal vultures so that your mother and you should be able to live comfortably for quite a while and . . ."

"Wait a minute," John R. interjected, "this sounds like Mom and I aren't a part of this new life."

"It's not that you're not a part of it. All this is a personal mission on my part. It's something I've got to do for myself, by myself."

"Excuse me for saying so since I've only had four hours of psychology, but this is beginning to sound a little nutty to me."

"I didn't expect you to understand . . . I told you that."

John R. jumped to his feet so violently that his large frame rocked the boat. "So Mom and Carrie and I are just history, is that it? *Adios, amigos*, I've got to finish some unfinished business."

"John R., you'll always be a part of my life. I'm not going to abandon anybody. It's just—well, it's like a sequence from 'The Twilight Zone' except I don't want to go back to being eighteen again. I just want to do some things I didn't do, say things I didn't say . . ."

"Sure, sure. And where does Doctor-Ms. Medoc—Maggie—fit into this?"

"Maggie? Oh, Maggie . . ." Hudson smiled, which caused John R. to frown. "Maggie told me you caught her unawares this morning."

"More like I caught her naked except for your shirt."

"Maggie is a real pain, isn't she?"

John R. scratched his head. "Hold on . . . That's my line, isn't it?"

"John R., Maggie is an annoyance to me like you can't believe. She's a very insecure person."

"Boy, this is getting really nutty, Dad. The doctor is a pain?"

Hudson corrected him. "She doesn't have her doctorate yet. Has everything but her dissertation, but calls herself a doctor for professional reasons. She's using this video project to write her dissertation. I have to listen to a ton of her sophisticated gibberish each day to make the video company happy."

"But what about the shirt and the neck massages?" John R. protested.

"That's part of her insecurity. She wants a man so badly that it's tough to listen to all her women's lib babble without laughing out loud. I tried to tell her to cool it. I'm a married man who's not interested. Each time I say something like that, she denies what she's doing and gives me a lecture about male ego and castration complexes. She is a genuine weirdo, I'll grant you that."

"Why put up with her then? Why not call the video company and tell them she's no help?"

"Her father is on the video company's board of directors. A few of the projects she's been on have turned out quite profitably, and credit for the success was given to her by clients who knew it would please Big Daddy. I'm stuck with her for a while longer, I'm afraid."

"What's so complicated about a videotape anyway? All kinds of people have video cameras now, taking pictures of everything from their kid's birthday party to pictures of themselves hitting golf balls ten yards."

"The equipment is not the issue. It's the advertising, the distribution, the hotel and motel arrangements, attracting customers that you can't get as an individual. It's a big business. Shooting the tape is only a small part of the whole project. It takes big money to make it go. There's a lot of selling involved."

"Including selling out what your heart knows is right?" John R.'s question was intended as a statement.

Hudson looked at his son pensively. Ordinarily such a statement would have been met with a sharp response, a temperamental outburst laced with strong words. This time, however, he was impressed and stung by John R.'s question. Softly, haltingly, he responded, "I'm tired, John R. Just plain tired. I'm tired of being on the road and seeing the same plastic plants in motel lobbies across America. I'm tired of hearing myself say the same thing day after day. If this video series goes well, if I can raise the money to finance and distribute it, then I can get off the road. Try to understand, if you can, that I'm not selling out. I'm being tolerant of Maggie and this whole process as a way to regroup and get back to a more rational way of life."

"I understand," John R. answered. "That is, I think I understand. Does this mean there's nothing going on between Maggie and you?"

"John R., I promise you there is nothing going on. I just have some things in my life which I've got to get done."

"Dad, you were the coach of the best basketball team in the state, number one in insurance sales for three years, and you wrote a book which went over one quarter of a million in print. What's left to do?"

"I don't regret anything I have done. It's the stuff I haven't done which still haunts me."

"Can you give me an example so I'll understand what you're talking about?"

Hudson thought for several moments, but did not disclose everything when he said, "I want to own a motorcycle, ride through the Rocky Mountains, and sleep under the stars."

"You got any other examples?" John R. inquired flatly.

"I'm serious, John R."

"So am I, Dad."

Gray storm clouds slid in front of the sun, allowing the wind to carry the chilly blue-green water's surface temperature to their bodies. Both shivered. They talked for ten more minutes before John R. went forward to hoist the anchor. Hudson told John R. he understood why he had dropped out of school and would like to talk more about it later. John R. said he better understood what his father was trying to accomplish and would support him any way he could. As they left The Pointe's cove they knew they had just lied to each other . . . Badly.

SIX

Dear John R.,

"Don't call me, I'll call you."

"I thought I told you never to call me here."

"If a woman answers, hang up the phone."

What other grade B movie lines have to do with calling? "The postman always rings twice." Was that a telephone or doorbell? I forget.

Carrie told me you called the other day. As you know, I am dallying my way across the country. Some days I drive five hundred miles and others only fifty. Not very structured for a former president of the PTA and every charity in town, is it?

Carrie said you thought your father was looking good but acting a little strange. She said you told her he wanted to own a motorcycle and become a rock star. That's a new one.

Is Mrs. Berger keeping the house clean? I know you're not. Does your room look like Hiroshima 1945 yet? Are you eating anything decent? Eat salads!

I'm tempted to call you sometime, but I don't want to talk to your father just yet. As you learned, we aren't in his plans right now. I've tried to understand what he's up to, but he can't explain it in a language I can understand, and I can't hear it in the language he is speaking. "What we have here is a failure to communicate." Paul Newman in Cool Hand Luke. Did you ever get to see that movie? It must be in video cassette by now. Get it. Those teenybopper movies you watch are disgusting. Can you quote one line from Porky's? If you can, I don't want to hear it.

I'm doing O.K., if you were going to ask. In fact I'm doing very well in some ways. Because you're not with me to fight over the car radio, I've been able to listen to any station I want. One played only religious music and had preachers. It brought back memories of when I was a little girl and your grandparents and I would go to church every Sunday. Only this was better because in those days I would just color or fidget. By the time I was your age my father had died, and Grandma didn't seem up to going to church anymore. Anyway, I never heard many of the sermons like the ones on the radio. One pastor talked about unconditional love and how God loves us regardless of what we do. I'm having trouble comprehending that one. I even laughed during a few sermons. I don't know if you can laugh out loud in churches or not. I was in the car, so it didn't matter. When we took Carrie and you to church on Christmas and Easter I don't remember anyone laughing.

At one point a preacher talked about everything coming together for good. Given the mess my life is in right now, I'm going to look into this further. There are Bibles in almost every motel room I visit. I'm tempted to take one with me. Would that be stealing? Boy, I'll bet it would test God's unconditional love if you stole a Bible.

Sorry to run on like this. I'll talk to you before long. I still feel a little confused, a little angry, and a lot guilty.

I do love you, John R. I'm sorry your parents don't have it together yet. We've only been married twenty-four years. I hear the first fifty are the hardest. "And all the brethren said 'Amen.'" (That's in the Bible too. See how smart I'm becoming?) Seriously, if you do pray, I'd appreciate it if you'd "say one for me." (Bing Crosby movie by the same name. Do you even know who Bing Crosby is?)

Love,
Mom

SEVEN

"And at the end of two days, ladies and gentlemen, you will learn the secrets of how to invest in the most dependableand precious commodity in the whole world—you! Yes, you!" he shouted. "It's possible to invest in stocks and bonds. You can put your money in speculative business ventures that may or may not pay big dividends." *Look at me*, he thought, *I can tell you about it*. "But none of those ventures can pay back one thin dime until you have learned to invest in yourself first. Without investing in you, how will you know when to buy and when to sell? If you haven't developed a confidence in your own self, you'll go through the rest of your life reacting to everyone else, never acting on your own.

"The secret to investing in yourself is as simple as the word itself—INVEST. You must learn to INTERNALIZE four major concepts so that they are as natural to you as inhaling and exhaling." With this he flipped a switch on an overhead projector, and the word INTERNALIZE flashed on the screen in bold red letters.

"Next comes visualizing." A large red VISUALIZING flashed on the screen. "Folks, nothing begins without a vision, a clearly visualized goal of what you want to achieve in life. Can you imagine what Henry Ford or the NASA space scientists would have accomplished if they didn't have a vision? Why, we'd all have come to this meeting in horse-drawn carriages, looking at the moon wondering if it was made out of green cheese or not. What's your vision? Can you see yourself with a new home? A new car? A better job? A yacht?" The audience chuckled. This was Olathe, Kansas, and a seventeen-foot bass boat was a yacht in this part of the state.

"Next comes energize." ENERGIZE flashed in red. "Have you ever seen a successful team whose coach calmly sits on the bench and reads the Sunday funnies? No sir! He's running up and down the sidelines clapping, yelling, flapping towels, throwing chairs, waving his arms. I know because I was a head coach for five years. Why did I behave that way? Because I had a vision of winning every game we played, and I was committing myself, my energy, to make that vision a reality. I've heard the saying 'you can't win 'em all.' You sure can't if that's the way you think and act. I want to win at everything I do. It only takes a little more energy. And at this seminar you're going to learn how to put yourself, your total being, into that vision to make it come true.

"And when that happens, when we merge the vision with the energy, we SYNTHESIZE." Hudson went through a brief explanation of merging vision and energy to create a synergy which would enable anyone to achieve goals they had never imagined possible in the past. He moved to TRANSFORM, putting all the thoughts and energy into action. Positive, intentional, goal-oriented action. He scanned the audience, making sure he had eye contact with every person in the room, which wasn't difficult since only twenty-one people had signed up for the seminar and there were three no-shows. He was looking for a head nodder in the crowd. A head nodder was one of his greatest group assets once he moved the nodder to the front of the room. The nodder would bob his head up and down affirmatively at every key point. Soon after the head nodder was moved to the first row, those around him would begin to nod, then those in the second row would start to bob, and by the end of the second day half the audience would be shaking their heads up and down. His best performance was in Albany, Georgia, where he estimated five hundred people were nodding like a pack of plastic dogs with spring-loaded necks on the rear-window shelves of cars.

The best nodder in the crowd tonight was a young redheaded woman who not only nodded but took notes furiously. She smiled at his little stories and didn't look away when he made eye contact with her. He widened his eyes and opened his mouth as if he were surprised at his own story. She widened her eyes and opened her mouth, a mirror image of him although a half-second behind.

Perfect, he thought. *After the first break I'll move her up front, and she can rally this poor flock to my side.* "Do you think I'm excited about these next two days? Do I sound excited? I'm currently talking at a rate of nearly two hundred words a minute. That's nearly twice my normal speaking rate. That's how excited I am. And yet, ladies and gentlemen, that's only half the rate at which you can listen. That means you're going to want to go someplace twice as fast as I can get you there. Am I excited about this group?"

No way, he thought.

"You better believe I am! The potential in this room is PHE-NOMENAL!" He stuck out his arm and curled his fingers into a make-believe pistol. The barrel finger was slowly, silently pointed at each of the eighteen participants. When he had finished he broke into a wide, toothy grin and said, "People, I believe in you." A long dramatic pause, more eye contact, then, "Let's take a break. Be back in fifteen minutes ready to invest in you."

He didn't have to recruit the nodder—she approached him. A jade-green sweater and pale white skin added emphasis to a thick mane of long red hair which extended to the middle of her back. She appeared to be wearing no makeup except for a trace of lipstick which had worn thin hours ago.

"Mr. Hudson, I can't tell you how thrilled I am to really meet you in person," she said with her right hand on her chest as if to hold her heart inside.

"Why, thank you. And your name is . . ."

"Dilts . . . Jasmine Dilts."

"Pleased to meet you, Miss Dilts." Hudson extended his right hand, and she stared at it, her own hand still pressed against her sweater.

"Oh, gee . . ." She blushed and stuck out her hand, but he had already withdrawn his. "Gosh, I'm sorry, Mr. Hudson. I'm just so nervous meeting you in person and all. I've read your book, and when I was a little girl we lived in Indiana when you were a coach. My father says you were the best coach that ever took a team onto the floor in the history of high school basketball."

Hudson tried to be modest. "Well, next time you see your father, thank him for me. I happened to have five good years as a head coach because I had some terrific kids playing for me. There are many great coaches in Indiana basketball, however. You're either great or out of a job there."

"But you were in the Sweet Sixteen all five years, won the state championship three times, and were runner-up once."

"My, my, Miss Dilts, you have done your homework. I wonder if you could do me a favor after the break? Could you move up to this empty chair in the front of the room? You're the kind of person who makes these seminars all worthwhile, and I'd like to have you closer to me when we get into the question and answer section."

"You mean it? Gee, sure, Mr. Hudson."

"And call me Hudson, please. Everybody but my mother calls me Hudson. *She* calls me John. My real name is Henry John Hudson. Nobody ever called me Henry Hudson, thank goodness. A few older people called me Henry J., but I've been called Hudson since I was two years old."

"I'll try, Mr. Hudson. And call me Jasmine because— well, because that's my name."

For the rest of the day Jasmine nodded at all the right moments, and ten of the remaining seventeen heads nodded right along. Hudson spoke to everyone throughout the seminar, but whenever he spoke to Jasmine she stared wide-eyed, still in mild disbelief that she was holding a face-to-face conversation with H. J. Hudson. Her admiration for him went back to stories her father had told her about the teams Hudson had coached when she brought home the book called *Invest in Yourself*. She hadn't intended to read the book at all. A client of the law firm where she worked donated the book to the office waiting room. Jasmine took it home because it appeared to be the right size to shore up a Christmas tree stand which was tilted too far to the left. Because of her father's reaction she read the book from cover to cover—the second book she had read since high school six years ago. She couldn't remember the name of the other book, but it didn't matter because she didn't finish it anyway. She remembered the cover pictured a young couple holding hands looking at a herd of cows.

Invest in Yourself had no picture on the front cover, but the back cover had an old picture of H. J. Hudson along with a short biography. The book was facedown near the Christmas tree as she was about to slide it under the stand. Her father thought it was a present for him and expressed his delight when he saw Hudson's picture looking up at him. Actually Mr. Dilts didn't read much either, but he did recognize Hudson's picture and thought it best to make a fuss over the book so as not to hurt Jasmine's feelings.

Invest in Yourself was never intended for the general public. It was written at the request of the Midways Insurance Company to be used in sales seminars for their agents. Hudson had been the top producer for Midways for three of the six years he worked for them, and the company asked him to describe the techniques used in coaching and selling which made him so successful. From there he was asked to give one-hour motivational speeches at company functions, and soon after Hudson left Midways as he began to VISUALIZE a career selling a product that he found more interesting than insurance. The product was H. J. Hudson.

At the end of the second day Jasmine had VISUALIZED, ENERGIZED, and SYNTHESIZED her goals. It was now up to her to TRANSFORM them into a new reality. She stepped up to Hudson at the conclusion of the seminar. He was rearranging the order of the overhead transparencies so they would be ready for the next presentation.

"Hudson," she said more loudly than usual, "I want you to know that I have developed a new vision for myself and I intend to act on it."

"Wonderful, Jasmine," he said trying to sound interested. "That makes this whole session worthwhile for me." *Truthfully*, he thought, *these last two days have been awful*. He was so pre-occupied with the video project deal that he had gone through the seminar on automatic pilot.

She looked at him confidently. "It's useless if I don't act on it. Page 126 of your book says so."

"Quite right. You'll have to commit that vision to action soon."

"How about now?" she said.

"I beg your pardon?" He hoped she wasn't suggesting what he immediately assumed she meant.

"I'm acting on it now. My vision is to become an employee of your company. I can type or file. I took a word processing class at the community college. I've done all sorts of chores around the farm. I can even tune a tractor. I'm very versatile."

"Well, Jasmine . . ." He smiled. "I don't have many tractors that need tuning, so I'm afraid . . . Did you say you could type and do word processing?"

"Yes. I worked in a law firm for three years. I'd give you the lawyer's name as a reference, but he's in jail for tax evasion."

"Jasmine, as it turns out I do need a secretary. However, I've closed that office and I'm working at . . . uh . . . at a summer home I have in northern Michigan."

"That sounds fine. When do I start?"

He was laughing now. "Jasmine, you are really turning the sword on me. I'm afraid I can't pay you what you may want."

"Gee, Mr. Hudson—ah, Hudson, I just want to work for your company. If I could be a secretary there, I wouldn't want much more than room and board."

"I should be able to do a little better than that. I could put you up in the guest room for the summer. My son is at the house too. In a couple of months, if all goes well, I could pay you a more competitive wage. I'm working on a . . ."

"You mean I got it?"

"No, I mean I'll be at this number in Kansas City day after tomorrow. Call me if you're still interested. There are no guarantees with this job, Jasmine. It may last through the summer only."

"Golly, I can't believe it!"

"Believe what?"

"This silly stuff really works. I did it! I really did! I invested in me. Who would have believed it?"

They met at the Kansas City terminal and flew back together. Jasmine sat in a window seat staring at the clouds and landscape below. She had only been in one other airplane—cousin Ralph's J-3 Piper Cub. Ralph tipped the little plane to its side when she was with him. She was frightened then because the Cub's door folded down and there was nothing to keep a person from falling out except a frayed canvas seat belt. The DC 10 was big and comfortable, and Hudson was sitting beside her, so she knew everything would go well with the flight. She was unable to eat the food served to her because she was too excited to even think of eating.

When she left home her father kissed her on the forehead in a rare display of emotion. Since Jasmine's mother died, Mr. Dilts had become withdrawn, spending most of his time doing farm chores by day and listening to the radio at night. The radio reminded him of the times he and his bride spent together on the front porch listening to Jack Benny, Fibber McGee and Molly, or Fred Allen. Radio today was mainly loud music and stupid people talking fast. Television was worse, with stupid people talking fast and shooting each other. He wondered where all the stupid people came from.

One of the smarter people in the world, he was sure, was H. J. Hudson. Mr. Hudson had spent seven years as an assistant coach teaching a group of boys how to play basketball by stressing the basics. By the time Mr. Hudson was made head coach, the boys were on the varsity creating basketball history in a state that thought basketball ranked right behind sex for pure excitement—except on Tuesday and Saturday nights when high school games were scheduled and the order was reversed. He and the Mrs. would sit in the front room listening to the games. Dilts worked in a factory then. He hated factory work. If it hadn't been for H. J. Hudson's great teams to distract him, he would have gone crazy.

When Mr. Hudson quit coaching to try his hand at insurance, Dilts quit his job in the factory. Dilts figured if Hudson could leave a job he loved and was so good at, then Dilts could quit a job he hated and was so poor at. Dilts bought his uncle's farm in Kansas, and although he never prospered like Mr. Hudson, life was more tolerable doing a job he liked.

Dilts never knew that Hudson hated the insurance business. In the first three years people bought insurance from him because they wanted to talk basketball. That was fine with Hudson because he really didn't want to talk insurance with anyone. The money, however, was twice his coaching/teaching salary by the end of the first year in the insurance game. He pretended selling insurance was like playing a basketball game in Indiana, where winning was heroic and not winning was the best way to get useless advice from well-meaning people. Hudson's district manager was a well-meaning person.

Dilts could scarcely believe it when Jasmine came home squealing the news that she would be Hudson's personal secretary. Jasmine had been company for him, not so much to talk to as to occupy space in the same room. He'd known she'd leave someday. When he was sure she was talking about the same H. J. Hudson, he kissed her on the forehead and turned away to listen to the radio.

The plane landed only forty-five minutes late, and a rental car was available this time. Jasmine nodded as Hudson explained her duties would include airline and rental car reservations in addition to the duties he had described on the plane. She added "reservations" to a mental list she had made. She told herself to write the list down, but was afraid to do so for fear Hudson would think she wasn't smart. So far she had nine items on the list, but couldn't remember the first two.

John R. was tossing a basketball at a hoop in the driveway when the rental car pulled up. He pushed a jump shot at the basket, but the ball hit the rim and bounced onto the hood of the car. Hudson got out and said, "You need a little more wrist in it." He scooped up the ball and tossed it through the hoop with a perfect swish, turned to John R., and signaled for two points.

John R. heard the net cords ripple, but didn't see the shot or his father's sign of triumph. He gazed instead at Jasmine, who was sitting in the passenger's seat smiling.

Hudson opened the door for her. "John R., I'd like you to meet Jasmine Dilts."

John R. extended his hand, and she stared at it uncomfortably for a few seconds. "Oh, I'm sorry," she said, "I'm just not used to shaking hands with boys."

"Another one," muttered John R. to himself as he shook her hand.

"How's that?" she asked.

"Let me guess," John R. replied, "I'll bet you're a doctor."

"Golly no," she answered. "Why? Are you sick or something?"

"Jasmine is my new secretary, John R.," Hudson interjected.

"One minute I'm taking a class and the next minute I'm working for the company. I can hardly believe it," Jasmine gushed.

"I'm having that trouble myself," John R. mumbled again.

Standing at the rear of the car with the trunk open, Hudson called, "John R., help Jasmine with her suitcases."

"Suitcases? I suppose secretaries don't carry their own baggage, huh?" John R. said to her.

He placed her cases in the guest room as Hudson showed her around the house. Coming down the stairs John R. heard Hudson saying, "I thought this corner of the great room could serve as the office. The phone can extend over here, and the typewriter can fit on the desk, giving you space to work."

"This will be just fine," she agreed. "I hope I can concentrate with that view in front of me. The biggest body of water this little Kansas girl has ever been near was the Mississippi River. Hudson, could you excuse me for a minute? I'm going to use the little girl's room. This is so exciting."

"Yeah, Dad," John R. said, "you'll have to excuse me too. I'm going to the little boy's room—mine." With this he turned on his heel and bounded up the stairs.

Hudson was unsure of the tone of John R.'s comment. Was it intended as sarcasm? Was he excited? Hudson didn't know. Over the past five years Hudson had become more adept at reading the intentions of strangers than those of his own son. He stood on the deck and watched the bay which chopped and rolled, driven by a cold north wind. The water was gray except for ribbons of white which flashed when each wave could no longer contain itself. The waves made a churning noise, then exploded as they hit the beach, depositing branches and twigs that were still being washed into the bay by spring rains. Hudson loved the bay even now. He had come to respect it, to be sensitive to its moods, to learn that the bay had a vision of its own which would not be changed by words of persuasion.

He returned to the kitchen in search of food. While eating a bologna sandwich he saw John R. walking across the front lawn, a stuffed duffel bag over his shoulder. Hudson rapped on the kitchen window with a knuckle, but John R. kept walking. Hudson threw the sandwich on the counter and ran out the door, across the lawn, and down the street lined with chopped trees. John R. was two hundred yards away from the house before Hudson caught up to him.

Hudson grabbed John R.'s elbow. "Hey, what's up? What are you doing?"

"This duffel bag's up. I'm taking it for a walk."

"Where are you going?"

"To the boat."

"To cruise?"

"To live."

"John R., I'm not tracking this. What did I do? Did I say something?"

John R. flipped the duffel bag off his shoulder and banged it on the street with a thump. "Y' know, Dad, for a bright guy you have as much tact as that tree." He pointed to a dead birch lying on the roadside. "Last week you bring in some woman who's going to coach you on a video project. O.K., I can buy that. Now you bring home a backwoods redhead who is going to be your secretary plus she's going to live here. Did it ever occur to you that the neighbors might talk? Did it ever occur to you that I live here too?"

"Time out!" Hudson placed his hands in a T formation. "Jasmine is only a secretary. If you're suggesting something else you're dead wrong. I've closed the office to save on expenses. She's working for a meager salary because she believes in me. She has more faith in me than you do."

"You're telling me that in one week's time you've interviewed, tested, and hired a secretary? And where did she get that name—Jasmine? It sounds like she was named after a perfume from K Mart."

"It's true I didn't do much interviewing. She was in my last seminar and was moved by the concepts. Her vision was to work for me."

"Her vision," snorted John R., "is to return to Kansas after seeing the Wizard of Oz. I talked to her for a while upstairs. There's less space between Mercury and Mars than there is between her ears."

"Well, aren't you the self-righteous one. Here you stand without a single goal for your life except to get up in the morning and stay alive until bedtime." Hudson's voice rose in volume as his anger increased. "Yet you have the gall to criticize and cut down everybody in sight. But what are you producing? Nothing! What are you contributing? Nothing! You can't even finish two semesters of college because the world won't play inside the tight boundary lines you've drawn for everyone else."

"If that's what you think, then I'm better off living on the boat." John R. hoisted the duffel bag onto his shoulder.

"You can't walk away from commitments all your life, John R."

"What commitments? You said it yourself—my only goal is to stay alive until bedtime. Six more hours and I'll have attained another milestone."

"You promised you'd help me get ready for the Memorial Day weekend. In a couple of days I'm going to have over thirty people here whom I've got to convince to put some capital into a venture that will probably be appealing to very few. Everything has to come off like clockwork that day, and you're walking out on me."

"I'd like to help, but I don't live here anymore."

"You going to pay me rent for living on the boat?"

"I guess . . . if you want. It's your boat."

"Work around the house for the next couple of days and the first month's rent is free."

"Will I have to mingle with the crowd and make witty white-wine conversation?"

"Tell you what—the street is still a mess, so if you just greet the people and park their cars so they don't have to walk in the mud, you can stay or leave. It will be your choice."

John R. paused. "O.K. But I'm living on the boat this summer."

"Will you consider coming back?"

"Consider, yes. Come back, no. You're right, I had no goals. I've got one now. I'm not coming back until I know where you and I stand. I have a tough enough time understanding myself. Now I can't figure either one of us out."

Hudson smiled. "Sounds like we can learn to invest in ourselves. I know an expert on the subject."

John R. said nothing, hoisted the duffel bag up, and walked away.

At the Post Office the next day John R. received a one-line letter postmarked from Denver, Colorado. It read,

Dear John R.,

Read Romans, chapter 8. It's amazing.

Love,

Mom

EIGHT

The next two days Hudson's nerves were on edge. He began several projects to make the house more presentable, but finished none. Fortunately Mrs. Berger trailed behind him to make the place clean, and besides working diligently at her clerical duties Jasmine willingly pitched in at tasks which required a decorative touch. This was welcomed and appreciated by Hudson, who had the aesthetic taste of a hermit. Jane had long maintained that he was color-blind but too proud to admit it. While he was not color-blind, Hudson was color-ignorant. One reason the summer home was done in stark white walls and natural wood tones was that it was one of the few combinations Hudson could visualize without turning the interior into a scrambled rainbow collage.

Jasmine selected napkins, fruits, flowers, and snacks for the party which added the right blend of colors and texture to the house. Mrs. Berger was cool toward Jasmine at first, but warmed toward her as the redhead's enthusiasm and energy was poured into the preparations. Even Hudson's moodiness could not diminish Jasmine's vigor.

The day of the party was warm. A pale blue sky with fat white clouds that looked like dumplings which learned to levitate provided the ceiling for the bay, which pounded its waves onto the sugar-sand beach. The red-orange sun began to sink like a ball suspended on a rubber band which could no longer hold the weight of the glowing sphere. The house glowed inside as Jasmine lit candles of many colors and heights. Almost as an afterthought, Hudson asked Jasmine what she would wear to the party. Until that moment she hadn't given it any consideration because Hudson's invitation really was an afterthought. She literally ran upstairs wondering which clothes she had brought with her, hoping she had enough time to dry her hair so it wouldn't frizz.

John R. stood at the edge of the lawn waiting for guests to arrive. He had done the chores assigned by Hudson for the past two days without enthusiasm or conversation. When each day's work was complete, John R. returned to *Angel Eyes* without saying a word to Hudson, Jasmine, or Mrs. Berger. Hudson had asked John R. to park the cars wearing a shirt, tie, and black shoes instead of his well-worn jeans and top-siders. John R. complied by wearing tennis shorts, a red knit marina polo shirt, a tuxedo black bow tie strapped around his bare neck, and black ankle-high work shoes without socks. Six feet, five inches tall, he looked like a clown who had been dumped at the edge of the road before putting on his face makeup.

As guests arrived, John R. opened the passenger's door silently, then bounded over to the driver's side without a word. When asked questions, he made hand-sign signals as if he were mute, which embarrassed the questioner into asking no further questions. When the guests were in the house he would floor the accelerator, storm down the street at breakneck speed, slam on the brakes, and spin the steering wheel attempting to skid the car into a 180-degree turn on the stone street. While doing this he cackled like a crazed monster. When the car was turned around, he very slowly drove it into a parking spot like an aged, genteel chauffeur.

John R. counted fourteen couples who had arrived, which was the approximate number Hudson told John R. to expect. A large black Cadillac looked like an inviting place for him to rest until the party was over. As he opened the car door, a red Corvette slowly made its way toward the Hudson home. John R. mentally licked his lips at the thought of putting the sports car through his spinning valet service.

Only a driver was in the Corvette. John R. bounded to the

driver's door, gingerly straightening his black bow tie. A smiling brunette in an off-white chiffon dress swung her legs outside the car. She held up her hand and allowed John R. to pull her up from the low leather seat. Long, dangling, circular earrings bounced as she jumped up onto her high heels. John R. silently brushed past her, eager to get into the car's cockpit.

"If you pull the same stunt with this car like you did the others, I'll kick you so hard you'll be singing with the Vienna Boy's Choir until you're forty," she said.

John R. looked stunned, then faked some sign language with his hands, eventually pointing toward the house.

"Oh dear, you're a mute," she said shyly.

John R. nodded affirmatively.

"Then I'll kick you right now," she said as she swung her leg backward. "No one will hear you scream."

"Hold it!" shouted John R. "What's the matter with you, lady? Are you nuts or something?"

"He's healed! It's a miracle!"

"You're a lunatic!" he snapped.

"Dressed like you are, driving like an idiot and pretending to be mute, and *I'm* a lunatic? It'll never stand up in court, John R."

"You know my name?"

"Took a wild guess," she answered. "Now very gently park this car where it can't get a scratch, then change your clothes so you look like a human being. You're my escort to this affair."

"I'm what?"

"Move it, kid, we're late. Can you fit into this car? C'mon, kid, let's hustle." She gave orders in such a commanding manner that John R. parked the car and changed clothes as ordered.

"It took you long enough," she said sourly. "But the results aren't too bad," she cooed as she put her arm through his and walked toward the house.

"You're one of those kooks from the video company, aren't you?" guessed John R.

"You're good, kid. Sally Jones, security." She stuck out her hand. "Lots of money here tonight. There's also a couple of ladies here wearing very expensive jewels who need protection. Keep your eye on the redhead. She may be dangerous."

"Jasmine?" he asked wide-eyed.

"Would you trust somebody with a name like that, kid?" she answered as they went through the front door.

Inside, couples talked quietly as soft music played in the background. An easel with a storyboard presentation about the video project was standing in the corner of the great room.

Hudson spotted John R. with a brunette clinging to his arm and smiled broadly as he approached them. "John R., I'm glad to see . . ."

"Hudson, I'm Sally Jones," she interrupted. "I've heard a great deal about you."

"Nice to meet you, Sally," he replied pleasantly. "John R. didn't tell me that you . . ."

She interrupted again. "He's full of surprises, isn't he?"

"You can say that again," laughed Hudson.

"It's genetic," countered John R.

"Well, you two make yourselves at home," Hudson said, clapping them each on the arm. "Nice to meet you, Miss Jones."

"Sally. Is Jasmine here?"

"Jasmine? You know her?"

"Only what John R. has told me. I'd like to meet her."

"She's over there." Hudson nodded toward the redhead who was passing snacks out to guests.

As they moved toward Jasmine, John R. said, "I didn't tell you anything about Jasmine."

"Cool it, kid," she answered. "You'll have to provide me some cover."

"Hi, John R.," Jasmine said with the enthusiasm of a high-school cheerleader. "I didn't expect to see you here. Boy, am I nervous or what? How do I look?"

"You look beautiful," exclaimed Sally. "I'm Sally Jones. John R. invited me here."

"Is my hair too frizzy?" Jasmine asked.

"A little," Sally answered candidly. "If you have a curling iron and some mousse, I can show you a way to settle it down."

"Could you? Thanks. If it doesn't take too long we could run up to my room."

"Keep an eye on things, kid," Sally whispered to John R. She kissed him on the cheek and followed Jasmine upstairs.

"Whimsical creatures, aren't they?"

"How's that?" asked John R. "Oh, those two?"

"No, women in general." The speaker was one of the guests. John R. tried to remember if he was the black Cadillac or the blue Lincoln. "Jay Edwards," said the guest as he pumped John R.'s hand. "I was telling your father that I liked your parking uniform. Showed a lot of imagination."

John R. thanked him without much enthusiasm because he was wondering if his spinning parking service had been detected.

"I notice you've recovered your voice too."

"Oh that . . ." John R. blushed. "I've been having a little throat problem." He forced a cough and cleared his throat.

"I used to park cars myself," mused Edwards. "It wasn't a bad job as I recall. I could study during the lulls. We used to race them like crazy when the customers were out of sight."

Edwards had a casual manner and spoke to John R. as if speaking to a fellow fifty-three-year-old millionaire with seventeen jewelry stores across the United States. "I got fired," he laughed, "for running down a customer's battery while listening to the radio. Hey, John R., do you play tennis?"

"Tennis? Me? Well, yeah, a little. Why?"

"Well, I just put in a new court and I can't get a partner to play."

"Well, I'm not very good," John R. answered modestly.

"Neither am I," said Edwards. "I'm just a hacker. My doctor said I had to do something to relieve stress. So far I've got a graphite racket, a pair of Adidas shoes, a bill for $20,000, and no one who will play with me. If I keep reducing stress at this rate, I'll be broke before I unwind."

Edwards impressed John R. because he was not trying to impress him. John R. found himself liking the casual manner of this stranger.

"Where do you live?" asked John R.

"The Pointe," said Edwards.

John R. stopped liking him. "Well, I don't get out there much, Mr. Edwards."

"Nobody gets out there much. The boys at the gate keep nearly everyone out. It's a crazy system, but if I give them your name, they'll put you on the list to let you in that day. Better yet, I'll come here to get you."

John R. quickly replied, "But I don't live here. That is, I . . . uh . . . I'm staying on the family boat this summer."

"That's easier yet. How about 2 o'clock tomorrow?"

"Well, O.K., I guess," John R. answered. He couldn't believe he had agreed to go to The Pointe. He began to think of ways he could get out of his agreement. "But I'm not kidding, I'm not very good."

"And I'm not kidding either. I dress like a tennis player, and after that any resemblance is purely coincidental. See you tomorrow then."

Edwards moved into the crowd, silently making his way toward the soft drinks. He smiled at other guests as he passed by them. Handsome with silver-gray hair, a yellow silk sport coat, light blue sport shirt and ascot, he was too obvious to ignore, yet quiet and soft-spoken so that he didn't stand out like some of the other guests. John R. was shocked at himself for agreeing to play tennis at The Pointe.

"Hey, kid," Sally said from behind, "you're keeping pretty good company."

"What are you talking about? And don't call me 'kid.'"

"O.K., O.K., don't get in a snit. I've been on the stairway surveying the scene, and you've been jawing it up pretty good with Mr. Jewels over there."

"Who?"

"Jay Edwards," she said. "He's got a string of jewelry stores from Massachusetts to Hawaii. Lives in a big place on The Pointe."

"With a new tennis court," added John R.

"You have been getting along. See that lady on the couch he's talking to? Move over this way," she said, pushing him gently in the side. "Take a look at her. What do you see?"

John R. saw a small, dark woman in a low-cut summer dress the color of lime sherbert with a white shawl draped around her shoulders.

"I don't see anything in particular," confessed John R. "Does she have cancer or something?"

"You're a blind one, kid. Look at those jewels. Check out her necklace, earrings, rings, and bracelets. That is a walking fortune right before your eyes."

Since Sally had pointed it out, John R. focused on Mrs. Edwards's jewelry. Her necklace and earrings were a mixture of emeralds and diamonds, each of the emeralds surrounded by a circle of brilliant clear stones. Her bracelets were bands of gold in a variety of widths and circumferences. An amethyst and diamond ring on her right hand sparkled in the light as she lifted a drink. By contrast, her wedding ring was a thin gold band, plain and undramatic when held against its companion pieces.

"Let's mingle," Sally said as she wrapped her arm in his. To a casual observer it would appear they were moving through the party together. In fact Sally steered John R. toward the food, drinks, and guests *she* wanted to be near. Her course was never beyond a view of Mrs. Edwards, who unknowingly became the center of the circular pattern walked by Sally and John R.

The noise level within the house rose as guests became more comfortable with each other. Bursts of laughter punctuated the rising and falling drone of the party conversation. Hudson moved smoothly around the room making sure everyone had enough to drink and eat, pausing to talk with each guest. Jasmine was carrying trays of snack food around the room, but rarely said a word to anyone. Her hair was combed back and pinned so that a long, flowing red mane dropped behind the nape of her neck. It was quite different from the tight curled mass which had circled her head earlier. She felt regal and was unbothered by her role as a servant because she fantasized herself as a princess within a castle. She smiled genuinely at each person, overhearing conversations as she passed by, but listening only to a song she was singing silently to herself.

Hudson and a video company executive moved toward the easel in the great room, preparing to describe the project to the prospective investors.

"Looks like it's sales pitch time, kid. Why don't you and I step outside for a while." Sally was steering John R. toward a door.

As they walked down the hallway toward the foyer, a large, jowly woman with blue-gray hair was entering the front door. "Kelly," she exclaimed, "I thought that was you, but I couldn't be sure. I didn't know you'd be here tonight. You didn't tell me when I was in the shop today. Look what you've done." The woman patted her hair gently at the edges. "It's beautiful. I love it. I'll be in next week for a permanent. Why do you suppose they call them that, Kelly? They only last three months. Oh well, I've got to get back to the party. Snuck out for a smoke, just like I used to when I first started smoking. Don't ever take up the habit. Bye, dear."

"She called you Kelly," said John R. as the night air blew across the cold bay water. He folded his arms to stay warm.

"Seems like a good idea since that's my name," answered Kelly, unperturbed by his confrontation.

"Lady, who the heck are you?"

NINE

She was Kelly Hoerner, a hairdresser at the beauty shop in town. She had overheard a discussion at the shop about the party where many important people would be in attendance—rich people, Pointe people. During the previous winter she had read Hudson's book. She thought crashing the party would be a great way to practice the principles in the book while rubbing elbows with the rich. Her estranged husband wouldn't fit into the charade. He was a no-good part-time carpenter, part-time fisherman, full-time bum who left her with nothing but three rooms full of secondhand furniture and a huge monthly payment on the Corvette. John R. provided her with a way into the house after she had invented her security guard scheme. It hadn't occurred to her that Mrs. Robb or any of her usual customers would be at the party also. After she had first spotted Mrs. Robb, she managed to stay clear of the fat lady until the accidental meeting in the hallway. The evening was meant as a game, an experiment in visualizing a reality different from the one she knew in the beauty shop. Hudson was right—a little vision, energy, and whatever else was in the book allowed you to reach goals you never thought were attainable.

All this was explained as she wound the Corvette slowly around the rolling, curving country roads which once had been logging trails. She patted John R. on the knee several times as she told him her story. He flinched every time she did it. She was a toucher, a person who placed her hands on others naturally. It came with her vocation, and it suited her.

John R. was the complete opposite. He rarely touched people, and he felt ill at ease when they touched him. His mother was a toucher, but he was able to avoid her by telling her that others would think he was a sissy if she patted him like a little baby. John R.'s aversion to touching put a serious block in his relationships with girls. He was never certain when to hold their hands and when to put his arm around a girl. He solved his problem by rarely dating. When the conversation with other boys his age got around to girls, which seemed inevitable and unavoidable in his college dorm, he figured that he had kissed fewer girls than most of his peers boasted having slept with.

Kelly said she hoped John R. wasn't mad—she hadn't meant to take advantage of him. He could come to the shop sometime and she would personally give him a free haircut. John R.'s mood swung from offended to amazed. Kelly's inventiveness was only surpassed by her boldness. She had a goal which was silly, but she acted on it. She had ambition and courage. John R. reasoned that he had none of these.

He told her about dropping out of college, how disappointed his father was because he had no goals. He didn't tell her about the confusion regarding his parents' marriage or his mother's letters because he wasn't sure what to say without having it all sound nutty. He did say that *Angel Eyes* was his home now, and that he was being rotten to Jasmine even though she was being kind to him.

Kelly listened intently to him as she drove, sometimes shaking her head to acknowledge his statement. Several times she patted his leg to let him know she understood. At a stop sign, Kelly looked squarely at him, her face heavy with sadness, her eyes damp. Nothing was said for another two miles when suddenly a pickup truck swung out of a driveway flashing its lights up and down furiously.

"Oh no!" shouted Kelly. "Hang on, kid, we're going for a ride."

She downshifted the Corvette into second gear, and the car leaped forward like a pouncing cheetah. The pickup lost ground, but kept its high beams trained on the sports car. Kelly floored the gas pedal. One of the rear wheels dug into the gravel berm, and the car swung sideways with the truck's high beams focused directly on John R.'s face. Kelly swore as she expertly corrected the car onto the road again.

"He's seen you," she said as she flipped the gearshift back and forth between second and third.

"Who?" squeaked John R.

"My husband!" she yelled as she stomped on the gas again. "He's half-crazy. Thinks I'm playing around on him."

"Can't we explain it to him?" John R. asked as he fastened a white knuckle grip on the grab rail.

"He drinks and carries guns. He doesn't listen. He's a nut case," she answered.

The pickup gained and lost ground as Kelly approached a series of sharp S curves. She drove the car hard and fast. The beams from the pickup swung across the road into the oncoming traffic lane.

"He's going to kill somebody," she sneered as she looked in the rearview mirror.

"Yeah, us," said John R. nervously.

"No way, kid." She slammed on the brakes, bringing the car to a screeching halt with all four tires screaming in protest. She threw the car into reverse and backed it into a pine grove. The lights of the car went black. Twenty seconds later the roaring pickup shot by the pine grove unaware of a red Corvette with one tight-lipped driver and one wide-eyed passenger.

Kelly exhaled a sigh. "We've lost him. He'll chase all over these hills tonight . . . Probably will run out of gas before too long. I hope he freezes walking home."

She restarted the car and drove directly to the marina. "Stay in the car for a few minutes," she commanded John R. "I want to make sure he doesn't come around looking for you."

They slid low in their seats, although John R. was much too

tall to look inconspicuous in a Corvette. Minutes which seemed like hours passed.

"I think it's clear, kid," she said. He reached for the door handle, but she grabbed the back of his head, pulled him toward her, and kissed him long and fully on the lips. "I had a great time tonight. Thanks. Sorry for the hassle," she said softly.

John R. exited the car clumsily, confused. He looked over his shoulder as he hustled down the marina walkway toward *Angel Eyes*. He saw a second pickup leave the bank parking lot across the street from the marina. He boarded the boat and sat in the stern shivering for an hour and hearing sounds he had never been aware of before in his life.

TEN

Dear John R.,

I've become a Christian. I don't know how to explain this in a way that will be understood, but my life now is more than a thought process, more than a feeling. It is a way of living so that I'm not trying to direct or push my way through life any longer. The tough stuff I've turned over to Jesus, and I'm letting Him do the steering.

Once it was my impression that a decision for Jesus was one in which lightning came out of the sky and a person heard voices from Heaven. What I'm finding within the community of faith is that it hardly ever happens that way. Instead, each day is an experience in which I run on the power that is given to me by God rather than on my own energy. Through His love for me I am learning and living a more settled life from within.

I want to talk with you about this sometime so that you don't think I'm a kook who's going to live in some commune in the mountains. While I am in Wyoming at the moment, I know God is leading me to a ministry that is greater than living in a commune. I don't know what it is right now, but I'll find out with His guidance.

As for your situation, I have learned that:

1. You are living on the boat this summer.

2. There is a redhead living in the house posing as a secretary. Class move, Hudson.

3. You and your father aren't speaking to each other, or when you do you wish you hadn't.

Don't ask how I know these things. "Ve haff vays uff making you talk," as every grade B World War II Americans vs. the Nazis film used to say. Did you ever notice that WWII was fought in four years and yet we've had over forty years of movies on the subject?

Take care of yourself. Are you eating correctly? How can you if you're living on the boat?

I pray for you every day. You are one of God's treasures in my life, and I love you.

Mom

ELEVEN

He was thinking of her every day now. A year ago he felt guilty about it. Now it was a daily reality for him, and thoughts of her were as common as washing his hands. He still had guilt-feelings, but for a different reason. A year ago he felt guilty for even entertaining the thought of pursuing her, for trying to find out where she was and whether that night was an illusion or an invitation. Now that he accepted daily thoughts about her, his guilt had been transformed from being sorry for thinking about her to a point where he was disgusted with himself for not being more public, more honest about his pursuit. He wanted to tell people that he once knew a nightclub singer who looked at him in a way he had never known before. He felt she didn't look at him as much as she was able to look through him. If he had a soul, he thought she had seen it that night.

As for her, she was radiant that night. A blonde beauty which he hadn't been able to forget for twenty-five years. By this time she was probably like him—married with grown children and worried about their futures. But if there was such a thing as chemistry, an animal attraction one person holds for another, then she had sprinkled a potion on him, and he had to find her.

He wanted to tell people he had a vision which he didn't create, yet wouldn't leave him. He wanted to tell them he wasn't driving himself as much as he was compelled. He wanted to talk about it to someone, but said nothing. The closest he came to disclosing anything was to tell Jane and John R. that he had to finish some unfinished business in his life. Jane didn't understand him and left. John R. did likewise. Little wonder, as he could barely understand himself anymore. Gloria Laurie lived in places unknown. Gloria Laurie lived in his head.

TWELVE

"I thought you said you weren't good," panted Edwards as he approached the net with his hand extended.

"I'm not," answered John R. as he shook Edwards's hand.

"6-0, 6-1, 6-2 isn't good?" Edwards asked as he toweled the perspiration off his head. "Not only can you hit shots with top-spin and backspin, when you come to the net you look like King Kong ready to grab passing shots out of the sky."

"And you told me you were a beginner," teased John R. "How many beginners know topspin from backspin?"

"I have taken a few lessons," Edwards admitted sheepishly. "I even got to play a set with Jimmy Connors as part of a charity event in Chicago. He only beat me 6-3. Against you I only took three games in three sets."

"Connors probably played right-handed."

"He did not!" Edwards pretended to be insulted. "He had to stay in the singles court while I could hit to the doubles." Edwards smiled and winked at John R. "In addition, he only had one serve per point, and every game I won generated $10,000 toward the American Cancer Society. Other than that, we were even."

They both laughed. John R. had enjoyed himself. He was good at tennis (the only sport he was any good at), but really didn't care whether he won or lost. Edwards was also more interested in the exercise than the score. On close calls they each favored the point to the opponent. "Nice shot" and "Well played" were said frequently as sincere expressions, not tennis etiquette. Their age difference was bridged by a noncompetitive attitude toward a competitive sport. A winner had to be identified only because the scoring system demanded it. To both Edwards and John R. the score was functional only to determine who had to serve and receive. Neither would ever become a club champion or win a tournament. Neither cared.

Over the next three weeks John R. and Edwards played three or four times a week. The guard at The Pointe's gate knew John R. by sight, but still required that he be identified so that a proper log of visitors could be maintained. While Edwards usually picked up his young opponent at the marina, there were four times when John R. rode his bicycle to The Pointe. A narrow paved road made the ten-mile trek from the marina seem easy to John R. Edwards, who was usually exhausted after each match, marveled at the young man's ability to ride back to the marina without any apparent effort.

After each match John R. was invited into the Edwards's home for something cool to drink and a verbal replay of the game's highlights. With five bedrooms, four baths, a den, library, and guest room, the Edwardses' property was mid-range as Pointe houses went. The largest home, reputed to have eight bedrooms and four baths, was one mile from the Edwardses'. No one was sure of the exact layout of the house, as it was surrounded by a large, locked, wrought-iron fence which even kept Pointe people out. Rumors were that a daughter of the owners eloped with an Italian Catholic refrigerator salesman and the family was too ashamed to be seen in public again. Even the domestic help who came with the family each season never spoke to anyone beyond the fence, further intensifying the mystery and the rumors. Edwards never spoke about his neighbors to John R., and the young man never asked questions about Pointe people, although Edwards was making him believe his earlier-held opinions were given too hastily, if not inaccurately.

John R. and Edwards held most of their replay conversations seated on cane-bottomed chairs in the kitchen. The black-and-white checkerboard marble floor and overhead ceiling fan gave the kitchen a soda parlor atmosphere. Edwards said he liked the kitchen because it reminded him of a drugstore where he had worked as a soda jerk. John R. had never heard of a soda jerk and thought Edwards was making another self-deprecating remark.

John R.'s favorite room was the den. It had a love seat, two large, black leather wing chairs, red tartan carpet, a well-worn green rocker recliner which looked out onto the bay, and the biggest stereo outfit John R. had ever seen outside an electronics store. Twin tower speakers six feet tall adorned two corners of the den, while an amplifier blinked red and green lights as music played. John R. itched to twist the dials to full volume—to "crank it"—and watch the speakers throb. Instead, the music was soft and mellow, reminding him of mouthwash at a dentist's office. One day Edwards pointed to headphones which John R. slapped on as he changed stations and volume, two hands working the dials feverishly. As he landed on a station which played rock music he danced by himself, bouncing to a pulsating rhythm. He looked around the room as he danced, surveying oil paintings of horses and hunting hounds. In one corner of the room a large cardboard carton labeled "Edwards Jewelers" was half-full of mahogany jewelry boxes which were elegantly glossed and polished.

Edwards laughed loudly, but all John R. could see was a broad smiling face with eyes which danced as John R. bobbed and shook to a tune only he could hear. When the song ended, John R. returned the amplifier to its original station and volume level. Still laughing, Edwards said he enjoyed the floor show. He quietly explained to his young companion that Mrs. Edwards was disturbed by loud music because she suffered from tinnitus, an inner ear disorder which was agitated by loud noises and crowds.

In all his visits John R. had seen Mrs. Edwards only once, briefly. The small dark woman had walked quietly to the library, picked out a book, then went upstairs without speaking to either athlete. John R. thought nothing of it, but Edwards seemed upset by her behavior and apologized, saying his wife was shy. The party at the Hudson house over Memorial Day had been a rare outing for Mrs. Edwards, who asked to go home shortly after the videotape sales presentation.

After one particular match Edwards asked John R. to go to the den and put on the earphones for a few minutes while he made three important business calls. John R. selected a Mommas and Papas tape, which was the closest Edwards's collection got to rock 'n roll. He "air guitared" through "California Dreamin'," surveying the room which was becoming familiar to him now. Edwards entered the den and silently watched his young friend, who had become less and less inhibited over the past three weeks. John R. strummed the imaginary instrument, rocking back and forth like an inverted pendulum. He smiled at Edwards and waved.

The jeweler laughed, then imitated the silent strumming of his partner. They danced and strummed around the den together, Edwards imitating John R.'s antics, but looking stiff and tight in comparison to the loose-jointed, gangly antics of John R. Finally the jeweler could not contain himself any longer, and he pulled the earphone plug out of the amplifier socket, flipped a switch, and freed the speakers to blow 80 watts worth of Chuck Berry's "Johnny, Be Good" into the den. Both Edwards and John R. increased the speed and exaggeration of their dance steps and "air guitar" movements. Edwards still looked like a penguin imitating a mongoose as he followed John R.'s lead, but he laughed as hard as he had ever laughed in the past sixteen years. By the time the song was over, Edwards was soaked with sweat and lying on the den's tartan carpet rolling with laughter. He crawled on his hands and knees to the amplifier to turn the music down.

"My wife, my mother, and my banker would not approve of my behavior," said Edwards.

"Your wife . . . I forgot," said John R. gritting his teeth.

"Fortunately they're all in Chicago today," said Edwards as he cranked the stereo back up and danced himself into a state of jubilant exhaustion while a singer teased,"B-B-B-Baby, You Ain't Seen Nothin' Yet."

John R. sat on the swim platform of *Angel Eyes* humming "That Old Time Rock 'n Roll" as he dangled his legs in the cool bay water. Jay Edwards was fun to be with. In fact, he was completely unlike John R.'s earlier opinion of Pointe people. When Edwards laughed at John R.'s antics, John R. didn't feel put down; in fact, he liked to make Edwards laugh. When they were together they seemed to forget the past and the future. Edwards never talked about his business, his neighbors, or even his wife. John R. never talked about school, his job, or his father. Especially not his father. Instead they talked about tennis and their inability to master the game. Both had lied about their lack of skills, and they were improving, but almost hated to admit it out loud for fear it would cause them to become more competitive, giving scores and calls more importance than they deserved. As he pondered his friendship with Edwards, a figure blocked the sun he was using to further his tan. John R. took off his sunglasses as he raised his head.

"Water's cold yet, kid. Doesn't warm up until August." Kelly was wearing jeans, an oversized sweatshirt, and deck shoes.

"Hi," said John R. He stood up on the swim platform. "What brings you here?"

"The marina's the only place in town that sells regular gas. I need some for a lawn mower. Did my alcoholic husband give you any trouble?"

"No. He hasn't been around. I don't think he recognized me."

"He knows it was you, and he has been around. You just don't know about it."

"What? How do you . . . "

"We can't talk now. Can you operate this boat?"

John R. nodded.

"He's out of town tomorrow. I'll be here at noon. We'll go out on the bay so we can't be heard or seen."

"But I'm on duty tomorrow," protested John R.

"Switch with somebody. This is serious business. I'll be here at noon."

John R. traded days as ordered, and Kelly was at the marina at noon as promised. She walked to the stern of *Angel Eyes*, looked around quickly, jumped onto the boat, and dashed below deck out of sight.

"What are you doing?" asked a shocked John R.

"Just move this ark out of here like you never saw me," whispered Kelly through the cabin doors.

John R. idled through the no wake zone, then roared the twin engines for twenty minutes until the boat was ten miles beyond the shoreline. He shut off the power and let the boat drift. Kelly came up on deck. She looked him squarely in the eye and pulled her sweater over her head. He gulped, wide-eyed. She had a two-piece swimsuit beneath her slacks and sweater which revealed a trim, well-developed figure. The slacks slid off her hips and were folded onto the passenger seat. John R. tried not to stare. He failed. Badly.

THIRTEEN

Hudson called information for the number of the nightclub in Cleveland. It had become part of a federally-funded urban renewal program. Seventeen booking agents in Cleveland and New York City said they had no knowledge of a Gloria Laurie. Still, he knew she was alive. He could feel her presence, he could remember her song, he was haunted by her eyes which looked so deeply into a part of him that he was unable to let her go after twenty-five years. She existed, but where?

A Honda dealer in St. Paul, Minnesota convinced him that riding a motorcycle was a simple matter of timing and coordination. The Aspencade model would be the ideal bike for a trip through the Rockies, proposed the dealer. Hudson was not sure he understood the shifting pattern of the bike, so the obliging salesman took him to a parking lot behind the store. On a 500cc demonstrator, Hudson zipped through first and second gears. In third gear he panicked as the bike picked up speed too quickly. Instead of backing the throttle down, he cranked it to full acceleration so that at 35 miles per hour he hit a parked Beetle squarely in the tail. Instead of a new Aspencade, Hudson became the owner of a severely sprained left wrist.

At his seminar the next day, Hudson visualized a trip through the Rockies in a mini-van.

FOURTEEN

She spread suntan oil on her arms, legs, and stomach, then asked him to put some on her back and shoulders as she told him about her husband. Served with divorce papers five days after Hudson's party, Kelly's husband had become convinced that John R. was the reason for Kelly's action. A fishing buddy of her husband's saw Kelly kiss someone in her Corvette. The friend, spying from a pickup at the bank parking lot, watched a tall man leave the car and board a Tiara named *Angel Eyes*. Her husband had been following John R. ever since. She had screamed at him that John R. was innocent of any wrongdoing, that she was ten years older and not involved with him or anyone else romantically. Then she made a nearly fatal mistake by saying that John R. was more a gentleman than her husband ever thought of being. He punched her in the stomach and slapped her face. He said she and her gentleman friend were living on borrowed time.

She shook her head and shuddered as she finished the story; the pain of reliving it had become all too real again. Until now she hadn't looked at John R., but she lifted her eyes to meet his as he stood unsure of what to do or say.

"Hold me?" she asked plaintively. He wrapped his arms around her, and the oil on her body felt slick against his palms.

"I'll protect you," he said without a clue how he would protect her.

"I don't want you involved in my troubles," she answered.

"I want to get involved," he said. "My father has been on my case again about having no ambition, goals, or courage. This will convince him I'm better than he thinks."

She looked up at him, still wrapped in his arms. "Your father is too hard on you . . . I know."

"How would you know?" he asked.

"From Jasmine. Let's go downstairs or whatever it's called on boats. I've got a few things to tell you."

Kelly and Jasmine had become quite good friends in less than one month's time. Because Kelly had offered to fix Jasmine's hair at the party, the redhead identified Kelly as someone who might be willing to help her with advice about shopping and the discharge of the many tasks Hudson gave her. Kelly was a lifelong native of the area and knew who to call for whatever service was needed. Kelly was happy to help, and Jasmine was genuinely grateful for the assistance.

Their discussions eventually centered around Hudson. To Jasmine he was the smartest, most powerful man on earth. Yet she confessed to Kelly that he was amazingly complex. At times she would break out crying because she felt as if she had let him down when a job wasn't done to perfection. He expected the best out of everyone, Jasmine said, but no one could reach the expectations he set. Hudson told her repeatedly that he had had a dream of coaching his son on a championship team, but the boy had no interest in basketball. Hudson wanted John R. to attend West Point or the Naval Academy at Annapolis. Instead, he loafed his way through high school and was accepted at a state school because the state was more obligated than interested in him. Even then John R. had dropped out of college in less than one year's time. Hudson wanted John R. to take one bold step, one great leap of courage, one self-initiated action that would take Hudson's breath away. But his son seemed destined to go through life in a listless fog.

John R. nodded as Kelly told him Jasmine's account. None of it was new or surprising to him except that his father was now expressing his dissatisfaction to others, to virtual strangers—red-headed corn queens from Kansas who heard the confessions of a father's disappointment with his only son, the failure. John R. had been taught that family matters stayed within the family. Now the teacher was violating his own rule. The thought that John R.'s life was being spread out before others was more hurtful than any of the lectures given to him by Hudson.

"I'll show him," muttered John R. without a clue how he would show him. "I'll do something so awesome, so outrageous, he'll keep his mouth shut forever." As he spoke, anger welled up until he was spitting the words out.

"You and I, John R., have a case of the hurts." Kelly put one hand on top of his, drew her face within inches of his, and smoothed his hair with her other hand. "We can help each other, it looks like. At least we'll have someone else to lean on. That's more than a lot of people get in life."

John R. said nothing, but nodded in approval. Inside he was seething with a rage he had never felt before. His temples pounded, and he clenched his fists. "I'll show him, I'll show him, I'll show him. I will. I'll show him, I swear."

Kelly sat on his lap and held his head in her arms as *Angel Eyes* rocked back and forth. She honored her part of the agreement to be helpful by *not* telling John R. that in spite of Hudson's complexities, Jasmine had fallen hopelessly in love with him.

Dear John R.,
Love is an unnatural act. It's really not natural to love another person. It's natural to only pretend you're loving them. I've come to discover this forty-seven years too late. All my life I've wanted to love people and have them love me in return. Consequently I would say and do things I really didn't want to say or do. I thought others would love me for it. Even with your father, I tried to be like him rather than like myself.

Now I'm learning about me as I learn more about God. Take man and woman for instance. Added together they make one fine person. Separately they are lost. And when each tries to be like the other, the whole point of creation is lost also.

What a shame it is . . . Just when I figure out how to be a better wife, I'm on the verge of becoming an ex-wife. I pray for another chance with your father, although I don't know if he'd recognize me anymore. The bottle hasn't changed much, but the wine has aged greatly.

Went to see an old movie the other night—Ben Hur. I recall when I used to think that Charlton Heston was the star of the show. Only one person loved others from his own nature, and it wasn't Ben. Or is it Hur? Whatever. I'll be at Carrie's in a week. Try to call me then.

Love,
Mom

"Hello. Ron? This is Hudson. Yes, it has been a long time. They're fine. How 'bout yours? Good, good. Say, Ron, I was calling about that time we were in a Cleveland nightclub in our senior year. We played Western Reserve that year. I don't know—by ten or twelve points, I think. Anyway, Ron . . . What? No, I'm in business for myself now. Ron, do you remember that night in Cleveland? There was this piano player who sang, and he had a blonde singer as the opening act.

"I'm sorry, Ron, I can't hear you. Do you have the television on there? What? Yes, that's much better. Right . . . Cleveland.

"What? I don't know for sure. I think you had a couple of assists. Eight? Really? Boy, you remember that game pretty well.

"Ron, do you remember the blonde in the nightclub? I'm sure there was, Ron. I *know* there was. You and Larry were teasing me about her.

"Who? No, I don't see him anymore. I don't even know where he lives. He does? Larry? Doing what? Him? At the college level? My son is thinking of transferring there. Maybe I should call him.

Do you have his number? Wait a minute. Now I've got one—go ahead. Yep, uh-huh. How long has he lived in Cleveland? No kidding?

"You're sure you don't remember that nightclub? I know it was a long time ago, but anyone who remembers having eight assists should . . . What's that? No, that's O.K., I've got to run anyway. How can you be watching basketball? It's the middle of the summ . . . Oh, taped replays. Yeah, great stuff, videotape.

"Give my best to Michelle and the kids. Yes, I will, thanks. Yes, I promise. Good-bye, Ron."

FIFTEEN

"Knock, knock, can I come in?" asked Jasmine at the of stern *Angel Eyes*.

John R. looked up from the cabin area. "It's called coming aboard, not 'knock, knock.'"

"Can I come aboard then?"

"No."

"Why not?"

"You've got hard-soled shoes on. No one comes aboard *Angel Eyes* unless they have deck shoes."

"Well, I guess I'll just have to talk to you from here then. Can you hear me all right?" She raised her voice to nearly a shout.

"Take your shoes off and stop shouting."

She removed her shoes, held them in her hands, and began to talk in a normal voice again.

"What are you doing?" he asked.

"I'm doing what you told me to do," she answered defensively.

"You really aren't a doctor, are you?"

"Huh?"

"Never mind, just come aboard." John R. slouched in a deck chair. Jasmine stood at the transom.

"John R., I want to talk about you and your father."

"I should think you'd be talked out on that subject," he snapped.

She continued, ignoring his sarcasm, "It makes me sick to see the two of you fighting."

"You don't see us fight, you only hear about us." He emphasized the word "hear."

She seemed to ignore this also. "I can't figure it. You're both such nice guys."

"He's the nice guy," John R. said bitingly. "He's got a wall full of trophies and plaques to prove it."

"He really is wonderful," she said. "I owe my life to him."

"Me too. Isn't he something?" John R. mocked.

"You're not serious, but I am. I've got a whole new outlook on life thanks to Hudson."

She was so serious, so sincere that John R. stopped baiting her. "Sit down," he said pointing to a passenger seat.

The pace of her delivery quickened. She sounded like Hudson delivering one of his seminar lectures. "Before I met your father I had no vision. Worse than that, I was timid, backward. I had a limited education and was self-conscious about it. Then I read your father's book. Better yet I met him, and he didn't see me for what I was, but what I could be. He sees everyone that way. He digs the potential out of people like mining coal from the center of the earth."

"Sing it to me Clementine," John R. mumbled to himself.

"He made me look into a mirror and see beyond the reflection. Beneath this red hair there was a person who could get work done . . . Lots of work . . . And well done! In the past six weeks I've developed a confidence I didn't think possible. Your father sets high standards. I'm making them all and setting higher ones for myself. I help him with the business, and I keep the house too."

She sat there looking so innocent, holding a shoe in each hand, convinced in her own mind that Hudson was a kind of Svengali or Henry Higgins. If asked to guess, she would have identified Svengali and Higgins as a comedy team from "Laugh-In." Hudson had indeed transformed her thoughts and heart. She spoke openly about her new thinking. She thought her love for Hudson was more subtle. It was the one lie she allowed herself.

John R. had previously believed that his father brought home a mistress disguised as a secretary. Instead, she was a secretary whose soul had become the mistress of his father's lessons and whose body was willing to follow in kind.

"So where's all this taking us, Jasmine?" he asked.

"I'm going to be the peacemaker between you two. You're going to come to a big fancy dinner that I'll cook. When we're done with the evening, you two will be very happy. And I will too."

"You think so, huh?"

"I know so. I have a vision of it."

SIXTEEN

John R. was on his way to the Post Office when he heard the squeal of rubber as the Corvette slid to a stop next to him.

"Get in, John R. . . . Quick!" she shouted.

"What? Huh?" He lifted one leg into the car, and she accelerated, leaving his right leg dangling over the door. He heard more tire squeals, looked behind, saw a pickup truck racing at them.

"Not again," he groaned.

"He's really flipped out this time," she said angrily. "I think he's on dope."

Not one stop sign was heeded as the convertible flew through town. The pickup truck roared right behind.

"He came right to the shop . . . Threatened to kill me! . . . Did this!" She pointed to a sleeve of her smock, torn at the shoulder. "I saw you and figured you could help."

"How?" he asked, pulling his leg into the car.

"I don't know! You were the one who said you would protect me."

"Bigmouth," John R. mumbled to himself.

They raced out of town. The pickup was unable to keep up with the sports car, but the curving roads made it difficult for Kelly to lose the truck completely. They were on a road which headed toward Westport Pointe. A fork in the road loomed ahead of them.

"Turn right here!" shouted John R. to Kelly, who was about to turn left.

"Why?" she asked as she made the turn he ordered.

"Just watch. I've been here before."

Within two hundred yards the asphalt road turned into a gravel-and-dirt lane. As the Corvette hit the gravel, huge clouds of dust billowed from behind. A rooster tail of dirt ten feet tall stood up from the bumper of the Corvette and swallowed everything behind it, including the tourist cabins on either side of the lane.

"Poof!" said John R. making the hand signs of a magician. "The truck disappears."

"It's not going to work," Kelly replied.

"Why not? He won't see us until we hit the highway at the other end."

She slowed the car slightly as they came to the final quarter-mile of the gravel road. A three-way intersection leading to a major county highway was ahead of them. John R. looked behind them and knew there was no way the pickup could see them.

As they approached the intersection, the pickup was waiting for them at the stop sign.

"Where'd he come from?" shouted John R.

"I told you it wouldn't work. He didn't follow us. I saw him in the mirror. He swung left when we turned. The road to the left ends here too."

John R. groaned. He had only taken one route with Jay Edwards, so he was unaware of the other roads.

Kelly was seemingly undisturbed by the sight of the truck. She downshifted as they approached the stop sign. The truck was trying to block the intersection as she came closer.

"We're going to crash!" yelled John R.

"Hang on!" she commanded. The Corvette shot past so close to the tailgate of the truck that John R.'s right shoulder flinched and he waited to hear the crunch of the car door against the truck. Instead, the side mirror missed the truck's rear bumper by centimeters. As they hit the asphalt highway, Kelly floored the accelerator, and the tires squawked in response to her orders for more speed. Amid the noise of the engine and the tires, two loud popping noises were heard.

"He's shooting at us!" she hissed.

"Doing what?" yelled John R. His body throbbed with excitement, and he felt as if he could run almost as fast as the Corvette was being driven.

"Carries a rifle in the truck," she answered.

The chase resumed. Up and down hillside roads, around sharp bends, past cherry orchards and inland lakes sped the car-truck tandem. Dust flew, tires barked, John R. shook.

Kelly was anxiously biting her lower lip. She had lost the truck quickly the first time. Now she was trailed closely and was unable to shake free of her pursuer. As she swung the car in a hard left around a sharp curve, a .22 caliber pistol slid against John R.'s foot.

"Does this work?" he asked.

"Yes. Do you know how to use it?"

"I can figure it out." He fiddled with the safety and accidentally fired a shot straight up which frightened both of them almost as much as the driver of the truck who was gaining ground.

"Good thing the top's down," she growled at him.

"Slow down a little," he said as he knelt on his seat facing backwards.

The truck came in sight past a curve. It gained ground on a straightaway. John R. pointed the pistol toward it and fired off five quick shots.

The truck swerved back and forth across the road. Kelly watched in the rearview mirror as the truck slid into a ditch. The cloud of dust rising around it declared the Corvette the winner.

"You did it!" she shouted. "You got him!"

"I was firing above him, I thought. I just wanted to scare him," John R. said defensively.

"You scared him good," she laughed.

"We'd better go back," he said. "What if he's dying?"

"No chance," she said as she revved up the engine again. "What if he's faking and has that rifle ready?"

"But he went into the ditch," John R. protested.

"He sure did," she laughed. "He sure did." She stopped the

car, cupped his head in her hands, and kissed him repeatedly, ending with a long passionate kiss. "I owe you," she said.

Totally confused and flustered, John R. asked with concern,
"Do you think he's all right?"

"I hope not," she laughed. "But in a small town like this we'll
know in a couple of hours. Be on your boat tonight. I'll sneak
down with the news."

SEVENTEEN

Jasmine planned every detail of the dinner with great care. She knew Hudson's preference in foods, his appreciation for floral arrangements and the smell of lit scented candles. Her mind played out that evening from beginning to end. Before the final curtain fell, Hudson and John R. would hug in a strong, manly embrace, then turn to her with gratitude. They would thank her for her concern and care. She would smile shyly, being careful neither to overplay or underplay her role in the healing process. Each of them would love her. Hudson would think of her seriously when his divorce was finalized. She visualized the entire scene and smiled.

"You down there?" Kelly whispered into a dark cabin.

"I'm here," she heard, seeing nothing.

"I can't see you. Turn a light on."

"I can't from here." Suddenly she felt a hand wrap around her ankle. She screamed, then covered her mouth with her hand.

John R. had lowered himself into the engine compartment, pulling the hatch cover over his head. He had decided to stay in the engine area after sundown in case Kelly's husband came hunting with his rifle again. From the engine's hold he could see everyone who walked up and down the pier without being spotted. If Kelly's husband came, John R. could pull the engine cover over his head. No one would look in the engine compartment for another person, thought John R. No sane person, that is. Then again, he thought, her husband wasn't what a sane person would label as sane. Before he could find a new hiding place, Kelly came on board.

"You took ten years off my life," she growled. "What were you doing down there?"

"Checking the engines," he lied.

"Let's go below. I've got some news that will make your day."

John R. sat at a dining table with a bottle of Vernor's. Kelly lay in a berth on her stomach, her eyes riveted on John R., who was trying to sip his soda, but was distracted by her penetrating stare.

"What are you looking at?" he asked.

"You. You're something else," she laughed.

"I'm not tracking you."

"You saved my life today, you know."

"How's that?"

"Haven't you heard? One of your shots went through the right front tire of the truck, and another bullet took off the door handle on the driver's side."

"What about your husband?" he asked anxiously.

"You didn't hit him, but you scared him spitless. He told a couple of his friends he's never seen anybody shoot a pistol so well. He's going to stay clean of you and me for a long time now."

"I did that? Really? I thought I was aiming high."

"Don't be modest with me," she laughed. "You didn't tell me what a sharpshooter you were."

"Good reason for it," he replied. "I'm not."

"Well, you're a natural at it then. I've heard that some people can shoot guns by instinct. That sounds like you. You must have a natural talent for it."

"Maybe so," pondered John R. for a few seconds. "Nah, who am I kidding? Those were a couple of lucky shots. I'm no good at anything."

"Hey, cut it out, will ya?" She slid out of the berth and sat next to him at the dinette table. Her hip and leg pressed against his.

"You saved my life. You can call it luck if you want, but I'm alive and my alcoholic, dope-fiend husband is cutting a wide path away from me, thanks to you."

"I did that, really?" John R. asked again.

"You really did. You're my hero." She kissed him on the forehead. "If I were a little younger and you were a little older, I'd tell you a way I could thank you beyond a kiss on the noggin." She lowered her head seductively and smiled at him.

He felt his face burn as blood surged through his cheeks. In the dimly lit cabin he was certain that his head looked like a jack-o-lantern. His embarrassment was compounded by his inability to speak. Her hip and leg seemed to press harder against his, and she continued to look at his face with unyielding intensity.

He tried to speak, but nothing came out. Pretending that his throat was dry, he took a long swallow from the bottle of pop on the table. He opened his mouth to say, "I," but gas from the soda rose from his stomach and up through his throat, and he burped out a long, loud "arrrrrrgh" instead.

Kelly erupted with laughter. His jack-o-lantern face brightened by 100 candlepower, then he too began to laugh. Tears ran down Kelly's face. She put her head on the table and laughed; she leaned against John R. and laughed until her sides ached. She rolled her head back and laughed some more. He too was laughing, but it was because she was howling so wildly. He thought to himself that the laugher was being laughed at for laughing, which caused him to laugh even more.

She slid away from him, reached in her purse for a tissue, wiped her eyes, and blew her nose.

"John R., do you know you may be the nicest, most innocent person I've ever known?"

"No, but burp me a few bars and I'll see if I remember it," he answered.

They both started laughing again. This time he laughed with more enthusiasm and less self-consciousness.

Another tissue, another eye wipe, another nose clearing. They looked at each other and started all over again. The release of the tension howled out from them like a wind coming down from the mountains. Simple movements and looks were met with showers of laughter. Unfunny behaviors were hilarious in the context of this moment. Tears poured down Kelly's cheeks again. John R.'s stomach began to hurt as he gasped for breath.

The tension was finally exhausted, and they smiled at each other. She took his hand in hers. "I think I've got a way to get your father's attention," she said seriously.

"How?" His good mood vanished at the mention of his father.

"Trust me. I know a way."

"Hello, this is Professor Sommers. Who? Hudson? Not Henry J. Hudson, the greatest basketball player since the peach basket was hung on a tree. Really? It's the same one? How long has it been? That long?

"What? Oh yeah, I'm in the academic world. I liked college so much I decided to stay forever. Right . . . I'm here at Cleveland State . . . Economics. Don't ask me anything about the stock market though. It turns out I can only teach the theory. You did? How much? Ouch! If it's any consolation, I did too, but not that much.

"Do I remember it? That was a wild night. There was a big bouncer after us as I remember. Who? Oh sure, the blonde. She was giving you the eye. She's here in the Cleveland area yet.

"What? No, she was just a local act who was an opener for bigger attractions. How? The Sunday paper had a feature on entertainment stars from the area with a 'where are they now?' slant.

"You're coming to Cleveland? When? Well, when you know for sure, you've got to call and stay here, not in some motel. No, no problem at all. I'd welcome the company. My wife is in England during the summer term with a group of students. What? Yes, she's one too. English Literature. She'll be disappointed that she missed a famous author. Will you autograph it for us when you come here? No, I'm not kidding. It's not Wordsworth or

Shelley. For that matter it's not even John Kenneth Galbraith, but it was fun to read.

"How's Jane? The kids? She is? When? You old dog. Nope, never had any. Four classes a day is as close to kids as we get.

"Hey, yeah . . . Thanks for calling. You'll stay here when you're in town, right? Promise? O.K. I've got lots of stories and even more questions for you. Right. Right. O.K. See you then. Good-bye."

She had never seen him in such a jovial mood. Prospective investors were rejecting interest in the video project, yet he bounded around the house like a cheerleader on a sugar high. He hummed songs and whistled tunes as he read the mail. She showed him travel plans which were tight and full of conflicts. "No problem," he responded casually. Return calls were placed cheerfully. Even invoices were tossed off with a carefree attitude she had never seen before.

During the six weeks she had worked for Hudson she had found there were two H. J. Hudsons. The onstage Hudson was dynamic, caring, compassionate, and sensitive. The offstage Hudson was rude, blunt, selfish, and moody. As his financial pressures mounted, Hudson's onstage personality did not change, but his offstage behavior became even more severe.

Jasmine fell in love with the onstage Hudson. She fantasized that she could nurture the onstage Hudson to spend full-time with her as well as with his audiences. His new vitality and enthusiasm convinced her that the plan was working. She really had no idea how or why, but it was working. In fact she had a fantasy, not a plan. That could not diminish her pleasure at seeing the onstage Hudson interact with her. He was so alive, so confident, that it became contagious.

She decided to tell him about the reconciliation dinner between John R. and Hudson one afternoon. Hudson had just returned from a golf match at The Pointe's course as a guest of a relatively new Pointe resident who did not know the rules against bringing

guests without having them approved by the committee estab-
lished for such a purpose.

"We're going to do what?" laughed Hudson.

"Have a dinner here . . . Just you, John R., and me. We're
going to talk nice to each other and stop this fighting."

"Then what? Will we hug and cry as the sun sinks slowly in
the west?"

"Well, sort of," she confessed.

"Oh, Jasmine," he howled, "you are a cross between an ide-
alist and a soap-opera director." The tone of his voice was turning
from jovial to cynical.

"It might work," she answered defensively. "You talk in every
seminar about putting some 'reach' into goals."

"I do. And I also say that we should start with a short-term
target that is attainable. Getting the three of us together in one
room would be challenging enough."

"What makes a dinner so impossible?" she asked earnestly.

"People make all things possible and impossible. John R.
makes it impossible. I make it impossible. And you make it
impossible."

"Me?"

"Yes, you. John R. has it in his creative little mind that you and
I—how shall I say this without it being offensive?—that we are
. . . uh . . . lovers, not business associates."

"He does?"

"I've tried to tell him otherwise. It's a silly idea, but he thinks
he sees more than that."

"He does."

"Say again?"

"He does."

"He does?"

"He does."

"Uh-oh. Jasmine, how . . . that is, I never . . . "

She saved him the trouble of searching for words by blurting
out her whole vision, including a romantic involvement with him
after the divorce was finalized. Nothing was withheld in her con-

fession. His new mood with its joy of living was due to her influence, she thought. She could continue to make him happy if he would let her try. She poured herself out to him, holding nothing back, so he could grasp the intensity of her feelings for him.

His light mood turned dark faster than a summer storm over Lake Michigan. The same intensity which drove fear into the hearts of the ball players who were coached by him rose to the surface again. His dark brown eyes danced and his nostrils flared as he spoke in a loud, punctuated voice.

"Now listen! Get this understood because I'm only going to say it once. You are my secretary, period! Beyond that there is nothing. I absolutely resent it when anyone plans for me without my involvement. I ask nothing of others except that they do what they are instructed to do. Beyond your secretarial duties there is nothing that I want or need from you. I am perfectly capable of handling my own life in my own way by my own self. Do you understand?"

She nodded her head.

"You're young enough to be my daughter. What in the world got you thinking such nonsense anyway? I won't have it! Am I making myself clear?"

She nodded her head again.

"My private life is just that. My son, my wife, and my life outside of the office are none of your business. None! The good mood I *had* until this moment has nothing to do with you whatsoever. You live in this house and you operate from it only because my office is temporarily closed. Get it clear in your mind that as soon as I reopen an office you will no longer live in this house. Am I making myself clear?" The volume and tone of his voice grew more menacing with each sentence he spoke.

Without looking up she nodded her assent. Tears began to well up in her eyes, but she wouldn't lift her head to let him see them.

"Now I'm going out for a walk. When I come back, I want you to tell me you've stopped thinking such nonsense and you're ready to put in a hard day's work." He said this in the same manner that he'd used in halftime pep talks.

As he walked down the road, the tears rolled down her cheeks like raindrops on a windowpane. Before her confession she was afraid he would laugh at her and she would be humiliated. The humiliation was present, but there was no laughter. None at all.

EIGHTEEN

"John R. John R."—she was screaming wildly—"come quick!"

"Oh no," he groaned when he saw her.

Kelly was running down the marina walkway, knocking tourists and boaters aside as she sprinted toward him. John R. was at the gas pumps, unprotected from any oncoming attack by her husband. Forty feet from the harbor master's cabin was too long a distance to sprint for refuge—unless he saw a rifle flashing. The harbor master's cabin was just lumber and wallboard though, and it had no weapons for self-defense. He hoped she had brought the pistol. He watched her bounce off people, pushing them aside as she ran and screamed his name. But there was no pursuer, no madman chasing her, no pickup truck anywhere in sight.

This made him even more curious, if not more secure. He hurried down the walkway toward her. "What's the matter? Is he after you again?"

Kelly shook her head no, then gasped for air. She looked and sounded like an Olympic miler at the end of a race. Gasping for breath, she lifted her head to him with tears in her eyes, exhaled loudly, then said, "We've got to get to the hospital. I think Jasmine just committed suicide."

The flashing lights were still a red-and blue blur on top of the EMS van and the village's only police car as Kelly's Corvette entered the hospital parking lot. The sirens were off, which added an eerie effect to the swirling lights. It was as if an opera were being staged, but no sound came from the singers' throats. The rear doors of the EMS van were wide open, while the radio in the police car scratched out incomprehensible messages through rolled-down windows. Bugs and mosquitoes flitted around a dome light at the hospital's entrance, dancing to the static of the car's radio.

John R. followed Kelly as she ran into the hospital. He had never been there before, but she knew exactly where to go. They ran past a pink candy-striped volunteer seated at the registration desk. Her welcome smile turned to a frown, and she shouted at them, "Hey! You can't go down there without signing the visitor's book."

Kelly confidently led them down sparkling clean hallways. She pushed open an oversized silver door, the rear entrance to the emergency room. Kelly slowly tucked her head into the room while signaling John R. to stand against the hallway wall. No one was in the emergency room except a fat male orderly who was mopping vomit from the floor.

"Psst . . . Herman, what's going on?" Kelly croaked out in a whisper.

"Hi, Kelly. She ain't here. They left most of her stomach on the floor for me to clean up though."

John R. started toward the door, but Kelly motioned for him to stay against the wall, which he obediently did. Kelly opened the door wider and stood with one leg in the emergency room and the other in the hallway so John R. could hear the conversation. There was no need to whisper any longer, but Kelly asked the next question in hushed tones.

"Did she . . . uh . . . did she . . ."

"Croak?"

Kelly nodded yes.

"No. She's gonna wish she did, but she didn't. They pumped her stomach like they were going for oil, but all they got was puke 'n pills."

"Anything you can tell me?"

"Nope. Puke is puke to me."

"I mean about Jasmine . . . how it happened."

"Can't say for sure. Best it's figured is that she and this guy she's living with had some kind of a fight. He took off on her, and when he came home she was on the floor. Dr. Johnson figured she swallowed one of everything in the medicine cabinet. The fella must be a cottager as he didn't have too much medicine. What he had lost most of its punch anyway. Made her puke a pile though."

"Can I see her?"

"No way. There'll be doctors and nurses all around her with more important things to talk to her about than anything you'll have to say."

"But it's important that I talk to her."

"No way. If you'll excuse me, I've got some puke which needs my attention."

"You're sweet, Herman. Thanks." She let the door swing shut and walked out of the hospital, signaling John R. to follow her.

John R. agreed that he should see his father for further details and lend support. Kelly wanted to collect some clothes for Jasmine from her room. They rode together without speaking. The only sound was the noise of the roadway stones clicking into the fender wells like a signaling telegraph key. Hudson wasn't home, but the door was open and they entered. Kelly went upstairs, while John R. scuffed around the kitchen where every medicine bottle in the house was lying on the floor, each bottle empty. Even a three-year-old bottle of Vicks Nyquil had been drunk by Jasmine in her futile suicide attempt.

Hudson entered the kitchen quietly as John R. stared at the bottle-littered floor.

"Some mess, huh?" Hudson asked, not expecting an answer. "Help me pick this junk up, will you?"

"I'm sorry, Dad."

"What are you sorry for? It's got nothing to do with you. In fact, you could say 'I told you so' and be right."

"I wouldn't do that."

"I'm glad. No sense looking back anyway. I thought she was the naive one and I was so sophisticated. It turns out I was as much in touch with reality as Donald Duck."

"How else can I help?" asked John R. as he dumped the last pill bottle into a garbage can.

"Is that your car out there?" Hudson inquired.

"No. It belongs to a friend of mine. She's upstairs getting some of Jasmine's clothes. You may remember her, she was . . ."

"Too bad. I need a ride to the airport tomorrow. I was hoping you could . . ."

"Airport! Where are you going?"

"My next seminar starts tomorrow night."

"Wait a minute," said John R. as he held up his hand in a traffic cop's halt sign. "Jasmine is in the hospital after trying to do a capsule version of hara-kiri and you're going to a seminar?"

"The hospital said she'd have to be quiet for a couple of days and they'll have to keep her for observation. There's nothing I can do for her."

"How about visiting her? How about asking her what went on? How about caring a little?"

"I don't think that's a good idea. She has some fantasy that she's in love with me."

"No kidding," answered John R. sarcastically.

"I knew you'd get around to an 'I told you so' comment sooner or later."

"Sure, sure, turn it on me again. I came here to help and you're turning things into another Viet Nam." John R. was shouting, and his fists were shaking.

"You want to help?" asked Hudson. "Go back to college. Set a target for yourself and hit it. Be an actor in life, not a reactor. Plan some work, and work some plan. Don't come whining to me about poor Jasmine. She's a mixed-up young woman, and I feel sorry for her. In the meantime I've got bills to pay, a company to save, and appointments to keep. You want to help? Take me to the airport tomorrow."

"That's sick!"

"No! What's sick is limping through life from one lousy situation to another crying life's not fair. What's sick is not knowing from one day to another what you're going to do except complain about what others are doing."

"Meaning?"

"Whatever you want it to mean."

"You want me to work a plan, huh? O.K., I'll work a plan." Tears were welling in John R.'s eyes. "I'll be an actor, not a reactor. I've been trying all my life to make you take notice of what I do. Instead, you only see what I don't do. I'll change that," he said menacingly.

John R. began to stomp out of the kitchen as the phone rang. He grabbed the receiver and growled a hello. He paused for several moments without saying a word, then simply pointed the receiver at his father. "It's for you. You're a grandfather."

Kelly was waiting in the car with a bundle of Jasmine's clothes stuffed in a pillowcase.

"I forgot you were upstairs," admitted John R.

"I came out here so as not to eavesdrop, but you two made it hard not to overhear."

"Doesn't matter any more," he said. "You and I are going to talk about it again. This time I want to do it."

"What's that?"

"Rob Jay Edwards's house."

The first time she had mentioned it to him he was put off by the mere suggestion. She said it was more like a prank than a robbery, but he was unconvinced.

Kelly had been invited to the jeweler's home to do Mrs. Edwards's hair since the little lady's ear condition was getting worse and the sound of the hair dryers and the noise in the beauty parlor were maddening to her. Kelly chatted freely with Jay Edwards (who did not remember her as a security guard) as he wrote a check complete with a very generous tip for her services.

Kelly sat in a wing chair in the den where she could see the jewelry boxes in the cardboard carton. Edwards noticed her looking at the boxes and explained that he sometimes sold jewelry from his home, so he kept a supply of boxes there. Each box was made of teak, mahogany, and ebony wood. A brass plate onto which the owner's name was engraved in Gothic letters graced the lower right-hand corner of each box. A gold-embossed crown which was Edwards's business emblem tastefully decorated the upper left-hand corner. Each box, worth $100 wholesale, was given to every new customer of Edwards Jewelers as a way of adding a special "Customer Is King" touch to the sale. Edwards bought the jewelry from one of his lowest-producing stores to give a boost to the store's productivity and provide a young, struggling salesperson with a nice commission as a morale booster. She said that Edwards had told her he had once been a struggling salesman himself in his earlier years, and he knew how much a boost like that could mean to a person trying to make ends meet.

Edwards chattered to her about his love for tennis and showed her the newly installed court. He complained that few neighbors played, but a young man in town called John R. gave him plenty of competition and exercise three or four times a week. "When he mentioned your name, he lit up like a Christmas tree," she said. "He really likes you."

"That's why I can't rip him off," John R. had protested.

"You're not going to steal anything. Sometime when he's out of the room, you take one of the wooden jewelry boxes from the carton. Bring it home with you, and I'll slip some junk jewelry in there. We'll bring your father down to the boat and tell him you decided your mother should have something nice since she won't be here this summer. Show him a couple pieces inside a box with the Edwards seal on the cover and he'll assume it's the real McCoy. He'll ask you how you got the money, and you can play as cagey as you want. Tell him it's a goal you set for yourself, and you made it without his help. Tell him you can achieve any goal you want and he should get off your back. After impressing your father, you smuggle the box back to the carton in the den and everything's back to normal."

"Why can't I just ask Edwards for a box?"

"You want a $100 handout like some kind of beggar?"

"It would just be a loan."

"You're missing the point," she lectured. "This whole act is like a magic show. It's all illusion. You've got to take a box to prove to yourself that you really can set a goal and reach it. Your father has you so beat down, you don't know if he's right or wrong about you. It's you that needs convincing more than he does. By showing him the box with the junk jewelry he'll be under the impression the jewelry is the goal. Only you and I will know that the box is the real goal. Presto! He buys the illusion and as soon as he does, presto chango, the box goes back to Edwards again."

"No harm, no foul."

"Correct."

"But it's still not right."

"His harassing you isn't right either. Look, I was just trying to help. In my job I spend a lot of time making things look like something they're not. Think about it, and if you want to do it, fine. I'll help you however I can. I owe you, remember? If not, just say so."

That was how she explained it to him the first time, and he refused. Edwards had been so nice to him, and the thought of deceiving a friend was more than he could handle. But that was the first time. Now he was desperate to stun his father, to quiet his continuous critical monologue. At first he didn't feel any better about what he was going to do, but as he thought more about it, Kelly was correct. He wasn't going to steal from anyone. He was simply going to create an illusion, play a prank. It was harmless, and it would accomplish his objective of silencing his father. Didn't his father want him to set a goal and make it? It was all too ironic, too perfect. He was going to do it and smile at the results. Presto, chango. Kelly thought the goal was the jewelry box; only John R. knew that the real goal was closing Hudson's mouth. *Life is just one illusion piled on top of another*, he thought. If he ever got back to college, he hoped they would study Harry Houdini in their Philosophy class. He was the only philosopher who knew the truth.

NINETEEN

"Hello, this is Professor Sommers.

"Hudson, nice to hear from you again. Are you in town? What's in Jacksonville, Florida at this time of the year? Oh, work. Never ceases does it?

"How's that? Sure, you can come here anytime you want. Next month or sooner would be great. Really? A seminar in Cleveland? Sounds wonderful.

"No. She goes by her married name according to the paper. What do you have in mind anyway, you old fox? Oh, I see. Sure, she might come to the seminar if you invite her personally. There's going to be one hitch, however. Her married name is Smith, and I don't know her husband's first name. I'll xerox the appropriate pages in the phone book and send them to you. You might even get lucky and get her after a few calls. What's that old story that says you're no more than five phone calls away from anyone you want to talk to anywhere in the world? Personally I never cared that much about anybody. If I couldn't get them in one or two calls, they weren't worth knowing. Can't give you much more to go on than that.

"Yeah, sure, I can hear the jet in the background. Don't miss it. Just call me and let me know the exact dates. Right. O.K. Bye, Hudson."

"So what's the score?" panted Edwards as he flopped into a canvas director's chair on the court's sidelines.

"5-4 and your serve," answered John R. while checking his racket strings.

Edwards mopped perspiration from his forehead with a large towel. He opened a cooler and took out a bottle of orange juice. "How about a swig of O.J.?"

John R. shook his head no.

"Pepsi? Seven-up? Vernor's? Water?"

John R. shook no again.

"What are you, part camel? I'm dying out here, and you're not even sweating yet."

"You're running me around pretty good. The score tells the story."

"And my legs are telling me I should find the doctor who prescribed exercise as therapy and have Jane Fonda do aerobics on his crotch."

The next game was played furiously, with game point won by Edwards on an overhead smash.

"You realize that tennis history is being set today, John R.?" Edwards said with a smile. "It's the first time I've taken the first set off of you since we started playing."

John R. answered, "I really never noticed." And he had never cared, but didn't say so.

"To tell the truth, I wasn't paying that much attention either. My wife asks me scores after each match. One day she said could have bribed Ivan Lendl to throw an entire match for less money than it took to build a court and get beat every time."

"Gee, I'm sorry Mr. Edwards. Have I won every time?"

"Yes, but never apologize for being good, John R. Be sorry for being lousy, inadequate, or unfit—like me."

"You're not any of those things. You just won the first set."

"So I did. And she isn't home today so I can tell her. What a hollow victory. Ah well, I'll have to win the next two sets also. For $20,000 Lendl might take a dive, but he'd never do it for $7,000. He makes that much getting dressed as a human billboard."

They played the next set with great energy. John R. dashed from one side of the court to the other to retrieve shots. Edwards drove the ball deep into John R.'s court with a new confidence, charging the net to volley winners. John R. lobbed more to keep Edwards away from an attacking game. At 6-6 they played a tie-breaker, which was won by John R. on a backhand passing shot down the line.

Edwards sagged in his director's chair. His shirt and shorts were dripping with perspiration. He slipped a headband from his forehead and wrung it out like a washcloth.

"Am I having fun yet?" he panted to John R. while drinking more juice. His hand shook as he lifted the glass to his mouth. The soft breeze from the bay was not enough to cool the heat bounding back from the asphalt court. Edwards's feet were beginning to blister from a combination of running and radiant heat from the court. Nature in the form of a blazing sun and thirty years more in age beat him in the third set as much as John R. did. Edwards limped through a 6-1 defeat, but was too drained at the end to care about the score. He wished he had agreed to play only three sets instead of the best of five, but he had wanted to get in shape as quickly as possible when he negotiated the agreement with John R.

Water rained from Edwards's body. Sitting still seemed to have no effect on the flow of perspiration which ran into his eyes, down his socks, and off the tips of his fingers. His breathing was labored. His shoulders slouched forward, his head parallel to the court's surface. He amused himself by watching a steady flow of sweat off the end of his nose form an increasingly larger puddle between his feet.

"Boy, am I ever getting healthy," he gasped. "A couple more sets like those and I'll never have another sick day in my life."

"You O.K., Mr. Edwards?" asked a concerned John R.

"Nothing twenty gallons of ice water can't cure. Are you ready for a drink yet?"

"Yes."

"A moral victory for me—I got a camel to drink. Come back in two weeks and I'll give you another. Follow me to my soda fountain kitchen," he said with a wave of his arm. "I've got pop, ice cream, popsicles, ice water, and air conditioning to soothe your battered body. Good golly, you aren't even sweating yet."

"I am," laughed John R. "Not like you, but I am."

"Right now there isn't a fire hydrant in the world putting out more water than me," said Edwards.

He opened the kitchen door where a cold blast of conditioned air circled his soaked body. With outstretched arms he emitted a satisfied, "Ahhh" as the cold air lowered his body temperature. He took one step toward the refrigerator, then collapsed into a heap on the black-and-white checkered marble floor.

"Mr. Edwards!" shouted John R. "Oh nuts! Mr. Edwards, are you all right?"

Edwards remained in a heap. John R. rolled him onto his back and continually repeated, "Mr. Edwards, are you all right?" as if Edwards would sit up and say, "Sure, no problem."

Instead Edwards didn't move. John R. jitterbugged around the kitchen unsure of what to do next. He filled a glass with water and threw it in Edwards's face. Edwards didn't move. John R. threw more water. Edwards still didn't move. John R. threw a third glass in his face, but Edwards remained still.

Oh great, thought John R., *maybe I've drowned him. I can see it in the papers. "College dropout drowns prominent Pointe jeweler on kitchen floor." It should make great supermarket checkout lane reading.*

Edwards appeared to stop breathing, or perhaps it seemed so compared to John R. who began to hyperventilate. He threw open kitchen cupboards as if they would have an answer to his problem. He opened and closed the refrigerator door, the freezer door, the oven door, and the microwave door. He looked in each of those places, as if they would give him a clue how to bring Edwards back to consciousness.

He ran to the hallway phone and called the only number he remembered. Kelly answered the beauty shop phone on the second ring. "Stay put," she ordered. "Keep him cool. Put cold towels on him. I'll bring a doctor. Oh—and tell the guard at the gate to let us in."

John R. was aware that the guard would not let anyone pass without an owner's approval, as Kelly had learned from her previous trip. So he imitated Edwards's voice as best he could. "I'm going to have Kelly Hoerner and a doctor here soon. Let them in please. They'll probably be traveling in a red Corvette. How's that? Oh, I'm fine. Well, not *real* fine, actually. I'm feeling a little, uh, low, and he's going to take a look at me."

Towels dipped in cool water were placed on Edwards's legs, body, and arms. John R. refrained from putting a towel on Edwards's face. He didn't want to suffocate him as well as drown him. John R. watched Edwards carefully and saw that he was breathing. Impulsively John R. looked upward and said, "Thank You." Kneeling by Edwards, John R. prayed for the first time in years. While not poetic, it was a heartfelt intercession to a God John R. barely knew. The sincerity of the prayer surpassed its clever use of words. It was the only prayer he had prayed from the depths of his soul since his mother had been hospitalized for a tumor removal on her thyroid.

He stayed on his knees as he heard car doors slamming. At the sound of the second door's thudding, Edwards opened his eyes, looked up at his kneeling tennis partner, and asked, "Do I look like a person suffering from too much stress? I mean, I give a new dimension to the term 'laid back.'"

"Stay still, Mr. Edwards. A doctor is on his way."

"I'm O.K., John R.," said Edwards as he peeled towels off his body. "I saw a woman marathon runner pass out in Hawaii on 'Wide World of Sports.' She just rolled over on her hands and knees first." Edwards knelt on all fours as he spoke. "Next she just pushed up." He started to stand, but crashed face-forward onto the marble floor. With his face turned to one side he mumbled, "Of course she didn't get up either."

The doorbell rang. "That must be Kelly with the doctor. Don't move."

"If it's 'Wide World of Sports,' tell them I'm keeping the floor from levitating. It's a new Olympic event," said Edwards as he lost consciousness again.

Kelly and a Dr. Johnson rushed into the kitchen, with the doctor firing a rapid series of questions at John R. as he checked Edwards's vital signs. An ambulance was called, then Kelly and John R. were told to bring a change of clothes for Edwards and to meet the doctor at the hospital emergency room.

"Will he be O.K.?" John R. asked with concern.

"I think so. It looks like dehydration to me, but we'll keep him for observation," answered the doctor.

John R. called the guard at The Pointe gate again. "This is Jay Edwards. An ambulance is coming here for me. Let it in please. No, I'm fine . . . Really . . . Just a little unconscious is all."

Edwards was awake long enough to hear John R.'s call. He laughed so hard at John R.'s last line that he passed out again.

"What did I do now?" John R. asked Kelly.

"It wasn't your material," she answered. "It was your timing."

The ambulance pulled away from the house with Edwards and Dr. Johnson in the rear. Inside the house, Kelly smiled at John R. and patted his arm in a congratulatory style. "It looks like you saved another life."

John R.'s perspective was that he had almost caused Edwards to die. Kelly and he viewed the same situation from entirely different angles. Each thought the other exaggerated reality.

"Well, at last our prayers are answered. He's made it easy for you to carry out your mission," she stated.

"What?"

"While I'm upstairs getting some of his clothes together, you go into the den and get one of the jewelry boxes."

"Kelly," he whined, "I can't do it. Not now anyway."

"Maybe your father is right," she sneered. "Maybe you can't accomplish anything."

He looked stunned. She had never talked to him that way. He stood looking at her, all expression gone from his face, although the pain was visible in his eyes.

"I'm sorry," she said. "I didn't mean to hurt you. Go get a box and meet me in the car." As in their first meeting, she spoke with an air of authority and strength. He did as she told him, and within minutes they were leaving to check how Jay Edwards was feeling. John R. was sure Edwards felt better than he did, even if the jeweler hadn't regained consciousness yet.

"It's only a lousy jewelry box," Kelly said consolingly. "You'll have it back in a couple of weeks at the most. Nobody's going to know. No harm, no foul, remember?"

She was wrong. The harm had taken place already, and it could not be undone. Inside himself John R. knew this was not a prank, it was not an illusion. It was an act of desperation. But it was too late to turn back, too late to change, for the betrayal was complete.

TWENTY

He was reading the latest letter from his mother, which contained a photograph of his niece. The enthusiasm of his mother was unbridled. She adored her new granddaughter and went into great detail to describe such unforgettable events as spit-up bubbles and quantities of formula drunk. Her new life in Christ was also mentioned. Since trusting Christ with her life, Jane Hudson exuded a confidence which was surprising to John R. Her letters made her sound stronger, more determined. She frequently mentioned the comfort she was gaining because of the plan God had worked out for her life. The baby was a sign to her of the new life she was living. While a baby Christian herself, Jane said, she was thanking God for solving the problems in her marriage and was looking forward to the way He would work out the solution.

This change in tone from his mother fascinated John R. She had always been a worrier, an artist who could paint dreadful scenes of death and destruction when Carrie or he would come home half an hour late from a movie. Now she was thanking God for solving her marital problems even though she was 2,500 miles away and closer to divorce than marriage. John R. reread the letter three times to make sure it was really from his mother.

Seated at the stern of *Angel Eyes*, he folded the letter and placed it back into the envelope. The jewelry box was hidden directly below him in the bilge portion of the boat. John R. had been unable to sleep the night he stole the box. Unlike the night when Kelly's husband was stalking him and he stayed awake with fear, this time he couldn't sleep because guilt refused to let him close his eyes. Jay Edwards was the one person who never pushed him to do anything he didn't want to do. The jeweler had again and again opened his house to John R. Most importantly, Edwards talked to John R. as if they were peers, friends. Edwards never talked down to him. Edwards asked advice, but never gave it unless it was sought. The millionaire jeweler was kind, considerate, and alive with a sense of humor. To honor all these traits, John R. stole from his friend and betrayed him for his kindness. Kelly kept telling him they would return the box soon, but that didn't ease the pain he was feeling.

The walkway was crowded with tourists and vacationers who strolled by the boats trading comments as they licked ice cream cones or bit into squares of fudge. The exception to the shorts and shirts of wild color combinations was a tall man in a black suit, white shirt, and black string tie. He held a black hat by the brim, so that it almost seemed he was using it as a steering wheel as he slowly passed by the boats. He stopped to read the name on each transom, looked at the people on board, then moved to the next. When he arrived at *Angel Eyes*, he stared at the name, then pulled out a soiled envelope from his inside coat pocket. His eyes shifted back and forth from the envelope to the boat's transom several times. John R. had been below changing into his marina attendant's outfit and noticed the man in the black suit as he came topside. The man shifted his gaze from the envelope to John R.

"Can I help you with something?" John R. inquired.

"You young Hudson?"

"Yes, sir."

"I've come to get my daughter."

"There must be some mistake," John R. replied. "There's no one on board but me."

"Not here . . . at the hospital."

"Sir?" asked John R. politely.

"I'm Dilts. Jasmine is my daughter."

"Oh, Mr. Dilts. Yes, well . . . uh . . . won't you come aboard, sir." John R. suspended his rule about no one aboard in hard-soled shoes when he saw the seriousness in Dilts's eyes.

"I expected you to be a little older," answered Dilts as he ignored John R.'s invitation.

"Sir?" John R. questioned.

"I heard she went off the deep end for you, but you look younger than her. I don't understand kids today, least of all the women.

"Least of all," agreed John R.

"Why she'd fall in love with just a boy is beyond me." People passing by were stopping to listen as Dilts was no longer talking as much as he was shouting at John R.

"You ought to know I came down here to shoot you," said Dilts with a finger pointed menacingly at John R. "What would you think of that?"

"Not much sir," John R. said softly.

"I hope to shout not much!" Dilts retorted angrily.

"You are shouting," John R. said.

"Wouldn't care for it if I blew your head off, would you? But if my daughter dies on your account, that's all right, huh?"

"No, sir."

"Eye for an eye, son. That's what I believe."

"Yes, sir."

"Is that what you believe?"

"Yes, sir . . . That is . . . no, sir."

"Which is it, boy?"

"Right now, Mr. Dilts, I don't know what I believe."

"Your whole generation don't know what it believes. You do dope and drink and sleep together like there's no consequences. But somebody's always got to pay. You hear me?" Dilts was shouting so loudly that the whole marina could hear him. "Somebody's always got to pay." Dilts reached into his coat pocket where a bulge stuck out prominently. Those standing near him scattered to either side. He produced a pint of whiskey and took a long swallow.

"Trouble is," he continued, "you foul others when you play your silly games."

A conservation officer who had been checking fishing licenses at the boat ramp made his way through the crowd of gawkers. The green uniform and badge looked official enough to the color-blind Dilts.

"Officer?" said Dilts.

"I've been listening to the conversation." Realizing he had no jurisdiction beyond wild game, the conservationist asked, "Could I see your license, sir?"

Dilts was just drunk enough not to read the patches on the conservation officer's uniform. "Don't have one," Dilts replied. "I'm not carrying a gun. I just wanted to scare the lover boy here."

"I think you've done that well enough, sir. Why don't we just move along now."

"We goin' to jail?" asked Dilts.

"Not today . . . If you promise to sober up and go home, that is."

"O.K.," said Dilts as he began to guide himself with the steering-wheel brim of his hat. "Somebody's got to pay though," he mumbled. "Him the son of H. J. Hudson himself. His father must be heartbroken too."

"I'm sure he is, sir," said the conservation officer, following right behind Dilts. "I'll bet you're right. No doubt about it."

TWENTY-ONE

Hudson was ecstatic! He had found her after making eighty-four phone calls to the Cleveland area from his motel room in El Paso, Texas. Eventually he found a relative of her ex-husband's who knew how to reach the former Gloria Laurie. It took Hudson's most persuasive manner to have the number released to him, which was his good fortune as Gloria maintained her married name but had an unlisted number. Hudson regarded his lucky streak as a positive sign, yet became as nervous as a schoolboy calling for his first date. He went so far as to comb his hair and brush his teeth before placing the call. Several opening lines were practiced aloud before he settled on one which sounded believable yet not too saccharine.

As the phone rang he stood, polished his shoes on the backs of his pants legs, then cleared his throat. The ringing stopped, and he was met by a husky-voiced "Hello."

"Hello, Gloria . . . uh . . . Mrs. Smith, my name is . . ."

"This is Gloria," intoned the recorder. "I'm not at home right now but if you leave . . ."

He hung up. It was her voice all right. The search was drawing to a close. Patience was needed now. He called every ten minutes for the next three hours, only to hear the answering machine dutifully repeat itself over and over again.

Gloria answered on his twenty-first attempt. The shock of her live response took him completely off-guard, and he forgot the opening line designed to catch her attention.

"Hello, this is Gloria," she said. Her voice was even huskier than the taped version.

"Oh, Gloria, it's you! Yes, well, ummm, Gloria . . ."

"Speaking."

"Gloria, I—that is, we—perhaps you . . ."

"Harold?" she interjected. "Is this another of your stupid jokes? C'mon, I'm tired, so don't play around or I'll hang up."

"No, no!" he shot back. "Don't hang up. It's not Harold. My name is Hudson."

"First name or last name?"

"Last name. But everybody calls me Hudson. It's like my first name too."

"What are you selling, Hudson?" she asked wearily.

"Nothing. I'm giving something away."

"Right . . . encyclopedias, and all I have to buy is a yearbook."

"No."

"An Amway distributorship . . . Or two tickets to the circus if I buy a third for an orphan from the Cleveland area."

"No. I'm calling long-distance."

"Long-distance means magazines. I don't want any more magazines." She sounded tired. "Good-bye, Hudson."

"Don't hang up!" he shouted. "I'm a fan of yours."

"A fan? You have a wrong number, Hudson."

"I don't think so," he said less confidently as he really did wonder if he had a wrong number. "This is Gloria Laurie, now Gloria Smith?"

"Yes," she answered cautiously.

"Gloria, I caught your act in 1963 when you were singing at the Cherry Tree Lounge. I was a kid in college then."

"You're a charmer, Hudson."

"You were appearing with Matt Dennis," he plowed on. "He wrote 'Angel Eyes.' You sang 'Fly Me to the Moon' and an upbeat version of 'You Made Me Love You' plus several others. I think 'My Funny Valentine' was in there."

"Hudson, is this a question in the entertainment section of Trivial Pursuit?" While there was a touch of sarcasm in the question, she was also complimented by his recollection, and her tone softened.

"No, I'm very serious. It was late winter or early spring, and the basketball season was drawing to an end. We played in the afternoon, and that night we happened to go to a downtown nightclub where you were singing. The weather turned unusually warm, and the place was like an oven. There was no air conditioning, only ceiling fans." He was speaking seminar speed now—fast.

"I do remember that night. I was sweating so hard my dress had to be peeled off."

"A low-cut white gown. You had a sparkling barrette in your hair."

"Hudson, you *are* a fan. I'm impressed."

"Perhaps you remember me. There were three of us at a table, and though most of the room was noisy, we were paying attention. Several times you looked our way . . ." He was now speaking at seminar speed plus one—very fast. While he wanted to say she had stared at *him*, he thought it was less threatening to say "our" than to use the first person.

"Of course I remember. You stayed for the last show, didn't you?"

"No," he said with disappointment. "The waitress said you wouldn't be around for the second show, so we left." He omitted the reference to Hector the bouncer.

"That's right," she said. "You had the beautiful eyes."

"Well, I don't know about that." He felt himself blush with embarrassment and momentarily lost his train of thought. "At any rate I've written a book and I . . ."

"Hudson, you clever devil . . . You're a book salesman. My first three books are free, and I only have to buy four more in the next two years, right?"

"No . . . It's not that way. I give seminars based on the book I've written."

"I've got it!" she exclaimed. "How to buy real estate without using your own money. You had me going there for a while."

"Honest . . . It's not a real estate seminar," he protested.

"What's the name of your book?"

"*Invest in Yourself.*"

"Stocks and bonds then. My ex-husband lost a fortune that way. I'm not interested, Hudson."

"So have I," he laughed weakly. "No kidding, it's not stocks or bonds."

"Why should I pay for a seminar that will show me how to lose money? I can do that pretty well myself. If I need a real expert I'll call my ex. He's got a patent on the process."

"You don't have to pay. You can come to it for free . . . My guest . . . Special invitation."

"When will you be in this area?"

"Two or three weeks. Maybe sooner."

"You don't have a definite date yet? Where will it be conducted?"

"Details are hazy right now," he stammered. "My secretary takes care of those matters, but she decided to leave." For the first time he felt a pang of remorse for Jasmine. Mrs. Berger had told him Jasmine's father had come to pick her up, and Hudson was truly sorry that he hadn't talked to her before she left. A rare moment of self-doubt flashed through him.

"Hudson, I still think you're selling something. I'll tell you what—call me when you're in the area. You caught my act, so I might catch yours. No promises though. I'm very busy."

"Still singing?"

"No. I gave that up. I played a lot of clubs, cut a few records, and had a couple of laughs. One morning I woke up and I couldn't stand the idea of working one more club. All my records started out slow, then tapered off. And the laughs didn't seem so funny anymore." She exhaled a long, low, husky sigh. "So I decided to cash alimony checks instead of paychecks. The pay was the same, and the hours were much better."

"Can I see you when I get to Cleveland then?"

"Are you going to tell me what you're selling?"

"Only lifetime memberships to the Gloria Laurie Fan Club. Honest."

"You sure won't get rich that way, honey. Where can I buy a copy of your book?"

"Can't buy one. I'll send you one in the mail."

"Hudson, you really aren't selling anything, are you?"

"Gloria, in case you haven't heard, the best things in life are free."

"Tell that to my ex-husband," she said as she hung up.

TWENTY-TWO

He delicately lifted the box out of the bilge and took it below deck at Kelly's insistence. It was wrapped in an oilskin cloth, then rewrapped in a small dark green plastic garbage bag. The box was highly polished mahogany with a rectangular brass plate which could be engraved with the owner's name in the lower left-hand corner and a gold-embossed crown, the symbol of Edwards Jewelers, in the upper right-hand corner. As the cover was opened, three shelves lined with a deep burgundy velvet unfolded. The top shelf had compartments for rings and earrings. The second held pins and brooches, while the lowest level had tray-like compartments for watches and necklaces. By itself the box was a handsome work, crafted to be admired in its own right, yet subdued enough so that it did not compete with the contents it was intended to hold.

Kelly lightly stroked her fingers over the smooth outer surface, then similarly touched the velvet interior. "It not only looks good, it feels good too," she said softly.

"Well, I wish I felt good. How long before I can get this back to his house?" asked John R.

"That depends on your father. When will he be back?"

"I don't even know where he's gone. Probably out recruiting a new secretary somewhere. I didn't even get to say good-bye to Jasmine."

"Guilt-feelings about Jasmine? I didn't think you cared for her," Kelly responded.

"She was all right. I'm sorry I was mean to her, and I wanted her to know that. But with her spooky father around I thought it best I stay a safe distance away from her—like at least a hundred miles or more."

"Well, when your father comes back, I have just the thing to add to the jewelry box to quiet his aggravation toward you." She fished around in her purse in an exaggerated style as if she couldn't find what she was hunting. "I know it's in there someplace," she mumbled with a wry smile on her face.

A small brown paper lunch bag was lifted from the purse. "Here it is!" she exclaimed. "Now, let's see what we can find." Her hand rattled around inside the paper bag with the same exaggerated style used inside the purse. "Could I have a drumroll, maestro?"

"For a piece of junk jewelry?" he asked as he obediently beat his hands rhythmically on the dinette table.

The sound of a cymbal was imitated by Kelly as she pulled a diamond and emerald necklace from the bag. John R.'s drumroll stopped immediately.

"That's junk jewelry?" he asked in disbelief.

"No way. This is beautiful. If you look carefully you will see it closely resembles the necklace worn by Mrs. Edwards at your house the night of the fund-raising party."

"Oooooooh . . . you didn't . . ."

"But I did."

"How?"

"When I was upstairs getting some clothes for Edwards."

"You rummaged through her dresser?" he asked in shocked disbelief.

"I didn't know his dresser from hers. Dressers are gender-free to the casual observer. I pulled open a drawer, and there was this mother lode staring up at me. Go for it, I figured; let's put Hudson into a state of shock as long as we're in the neighborhood."

"Why?"

"I figured, why should you be the only one to take a risk.

You've taken plenty for me, so I'd take one for you. We're part-
ners, remember?"

"We'll share a cell together, you mean. Good grief, Kelly, stuff
like that's going to be missed."

She said whimsically, "I don't think so. There was so much
jewelry in her drawer she wouldn't miss it for weeks. Besides,
Mrs. Edwards will be gone for the next two weeks. Inside beauty
parlor knowledge. Trust me."

"Do you think my father is going to believe I saved enough to
buy this on a minimum-wage job plus tips?" He took the necklace from her and held it between his thumb and forefinger as if
he were holding a dead mouse by the tail.

"Tell him you skipped lunches or that you got a big tip or that
Edwards gave you a special deal. Make something up. You're creative. You'll come up with something. Besides, men are stupid
when it comes to jewelry. Your father wears one of those generic
plastic watches. He'll know this necklace isn't cheap, but he won't
be close on the cost."

"How much do you think it's worth?"

"See what I mean?"

"I'm no expert. That's why I'm asking."

"Five figures for sure. Maybe six. Depends on the clarity of the
diamonds and the inclusions in the emeralds."

"F-f-f-five, maybe six figures?" He held the necklace in both
hands as if he were cradling a newborn baby. "I am in big trouble.
BIG trouble."

"John R.," she said wrapping her arms around his waist, "if
there's trouble we're in it together, not just you alone. This is
going to work out. Think positive."

"I positively think I am in BIG trouble," he groaned.

She drew closer to him, looked up into his eyes, and said softly,
"You've been chased by a drunk, shot at, thrown out of your
house, and have rescued a guy from heat stroke. This will be
smooth sailing compared to all that."

He looked at her without expression. She pressed against
him, her head against his chest. She squeezed him tightly around

the waist and whispered in a husky voice, "What are you thinking?"

"I was just hoping that if I go back to school next fall the English professor doesn't make me write a paper on how I spent my summer vacation."

They laughed long and hard, but continued to hold on to each other. When the laughter subsided, he kissed her. They clung to each other, kissing, touching, and grabbing in a fashion John R. had never known before. Once again Kelly provided him with the guidance he needed when he became confused about what to do next.

TWENTY-THREE

Hudson drove back from the airport on the narrow two-lane road which bordered the bay. Not only did he drive so slowly that traffic backed up behind him, he stopped along the way to view the beauty of the water and its surroundings. Dozens of white sails were sprinkled against the blue-green water, while wisps of white clouds stretched themselves thin overhead. There was very little breeze, and the sailboats were sitting still while their patient crews waited for precious puffs of wind to propel them forward with nearly imperceptible movement.

Sitting on a roadside bench beneath a shady cedar tree, Hudson allowed the peaceful scene to be absorbed. The serenity and beauty calmed him, and he was aware that the washing sound of the rippling waves against the beach splashed their magic on him like an auditory tranquilizer. He promised himself a vacation soon so he could unwind with the encouragement of this massive body of water which he loved so much.

The vacation would have to wait for a while, however. Before leaving El Paso he had received a call from Strategic Films, Inc. that two venture capitalists had expressed an interest in his video-tape educational series within the past week. The project which had seemed doomed now appeared to be a sure thing. One of the investors was Jay Edwards.

After receiving the news, Hudson's emotions went through wild swings which confused him. He expected to be elated, perhaps even relieved. Instead a sense of guilt washed over him larger than any wave he had encountered on the big lake. Edwards had been befriended by John R., yet Hudson had barely spoken to his son all summer. Surely John R. had had a positive influence on the jeweler, and that was why Edwards decided to risk some money in a field completely foreign to the world of precious stones and metals.

Gloria Laurie had been located, yet Hudson's excitement was cooled by haunting regrets about his treatment of Jane, who still took the blame for their marital problems, including the financial difficulties. Compounding his displeasure with himself was the knowledge that he had not seen his granddaughter, nor had he even held a conversation of any length with Carrie since the birth of the baby. Hudson found himself immobilized by his situation, a condition he ridiculed in his seminars. He wanted to see Gloria Laurie soon, to explore the mystery of an evening which had haunted him for years. Attempts at family conversations and reconciliation would only hurt those around him if his relationship with Gloria were discovered. By contrast, he was aware that he was becoming a person who was so self-centered and callous toward his family that he began to dislike himself with an intensity usually reserved for others. Hudson's dilemma was that an expression of love toward his family could bring pain to them, yet not expressing that love brought pain also. Neither choice seemed acceptable, so he chose an alternative which could give the appearance of closeness without the emotional investment. He gave gifts.

Granddaughter received a high chair, bassinet, crib, toys, and enough clothes so she would not have to wear the same outfit for three months. Carrie got flowers, candy, and a complete video camera outfit to record the progress of the baby. Jane's presents took the form of flowers and an entire wardrobe suitable for California weather. In the trunk of the car were John R.'s portable stereo system, a Sony Walkman, and a five-inch AC-DC color television set.

"What are you doing here?" John R. asked.
"A warm welcome to you too," Hudson responded.
"I mean, I didn't expect to see you sitting on the back of the

boat." John R. had just finished his shift at the marina. Business had been brisk, the weather was hot, and he had stumbled his way to *Angel Eyes* unaware of his father stretched out on a lounge chair.

"Great day," Hudson said casually. "Temperature hit 86 degrees. I've been catching some rays."

"You came here to give me a weather report?" answered John R. as he pulled off his perspiration-soaked marina shirt. "What was the relative humidity?"

"John R., let's take 'er out and tie up at Montrose for dinner."

"It'll take us an hour to get there. We'll need reservations. There must be three million tourists here this summer."

"I've made reservations. You've got to be hungry. Your mother will never forgive me if you don't eat right."

"Have you talked to her?" John R. asked eagerly. He hoped his father's visit was an announcement that the silliness between his parents was over.

"As a matter of fact I talked to Carrie and your mother earlier today."

"And?"

"They're fine. I think I woke them up. I forgot about the time change."

"That's it?"

"No. They also thanked me for the presents. Speaking of presents, I have a surprise or two for you." Hudson moved to the engine cover and began to lift it.

"What are you doing?" shouted John R.

"I put something down here," Hudson said defensively. "Don't worry, I won't touch the engines."

Hudson reached into the engine's hold with John R. watching intently. John R. had taped the box and the necklace into a dark corner of the hold. He was the only person who knew the location, which was too obvious to be suspected as a hiding place and yet was vulnerable to discovery. John R. momentarily wondered if his father was wise to what Kelly and he had done. He braced himself for the worst.

"What's this?" John R. said with relief as Hudson held a large radio in his hand.

"It's a boom box . . . A ghetto blaster in some circles . . . A stereo radio with cassette player to the older set. Do you like it?"

"Sure, it's great. What's the occasion?"

"Just a present," Hudson lied. "It doesn't have any reason behind it. And now for act two."

Hudson extracted a Sony Walkman from the hold, followed by act three in the form of a miniature color TV.

"I'm getting hungry. What do you say we cast off?" Hudson was happy with himself, although he was a little disappointed with John R.'s lack of enthusiasm. Their strained relationship was the reason John R. contained himself, Hudson reasoned. At least they weren't shouting at each other, and one hour of civilized conversation had cost Hudson only $1,176 plus tax.

Dinner was tasty if not spirited. The gulf between them had been widened by recent events which neither cared to discuss. In truth, their distance had begun five years earlier when Hudson began to travel more and listen less. Time and silence acted as agents of erosion which ground away at the substance which existed between them. It would be convenient to say that Hudson's preoccupation with Gloria Laurie and his callous behavior toward Jasmine (not to mention his own family) was a key factor in their inability to hold an in-depth conversation. Or it could be said that John R.'s theft and lack of direction forced them to discuss subjects limited to weather, boats, and types of tennis rackets. But the fact was that recent events were merely exaggerations of their inability to discuss any subject for any length of time without one of them ending up hurt or angry.

Each was uncomfortable throughout the dinner, although both pretended that the conversation was slow because they concentrated on the food. Both were relieved when the bill came. They decided to leave immediately, as there was a large number of people waiting for tables. The real reason they left so quickly, however, is that they had nothing to say to each other and they both knew it. Sitting at a table in the middle of a busy restaurant amplified the conversations of other patrons and reminded them of how little they could discuss.

Each did have an agenda he wanted to cover, however. Hudson untied *Angel Eyes* from her mooring by the restaurant and guided her out onto the bay. The sky was a mixture of purple, gray, and gold as the sun began its slow descent on the warm summer evening. Darkness would not come until nearly 10 o'clock, as the Michigan summer days reluctantly passed away so their beauty would not be quickly forgotten. *Angel Eyes'* wake was the only movement on the bay. The light breeze of the afternoon had faded so that the bay itself looked like a long blue table surrounded by guests dressed in hues of green and brown.

Ten miles from the Westport Marina, Hudson backed down the engines to an idle and finally to a complete stop. Neither said a word, although John R. knew that his father would spend some time surveying the bay and the awesome beauty which surrounded him. While he had traveled extensively, Hudson had never seen any sight which touched him more deeply than the clear blue waters and green hills which graced northern Michigan. John R. knew that his father was going to speak to him eventually, but he enjoyed watching Hudson stare at the scenery as if he were discovering it for the first time.

"I never tire of this place," Hudson said.

"I can tell." John R. smiled at his father's restatement of the obvious.

"John R., I've been doing a little soul searching lately. I'd like to share some of it with you, ask your thoughts, say thanks as appropriate."

"This sounds heavy to me."

"In a way it is. Some of this hangs heavy on my heart. You were correct about Jasmine all along. She was impressionable, and I took advantage of that. Not intentionally . . . then again, maybe so—I just don't know. At any rate you were also right that I shouldn't have left while she was in the hospital. I hated to admit what a mistake I had made. Going to the hospital would have been a bad scene for me. Not going, as it turns out, was just as bad, maybe worse."

"If you're apologizing, it's to the wrong person."

"No, I owe you an apology too. And you owe me an explanation—a big one."

"Explain what?" he asked as if he didn't know. John R. felt his face redden. He had already been discovered. But how?

"Why did you do it?" Hudson asked seriously.

"Well, I really didn't want to . . . That is, I wanted to impress you, so . . ."

"You did that for sure. What in the world made you do it, I'll never understand. Everyone in town is talking about it, I'm told."

"They are?"

"Yes, and I would probably never have known except for the honesty of Scotty Buchanan in slip space forty-one."

"He knows?"

"He was there when it happened, he said."

"He was? Where?"

"Sitting on the back of his boat. He said the big fellow in the black suit threatened you. Scotty wouldn't go into all the details, to spare my feelings, so I grabbed lunch at Humphrey's. No one there knew me, and I got the full story. Apparently Mr. Dilts thought you and Jasmine . . ."

"Oh that," John R. sighed. "That was no big deal."

"John R., it was. Why did you let him accuse you? Considering the way I treated you before I left, you could have told him the truth and taken the heat off of you."

"It wouldn't have proven anything. Besides, Jasmine told me how he idolizes you. He was one of your biggest fans in Indiana, so even if I told him what took place, he wouldn't have believed it. Besides, I was too scared to argue. If he thought she went goofy over me, that was what I thought too. Anything he said sounded perfectly fine to me. He had a bulge in his coat that looked like an old Remington six-shooter to me. Luckily it was an Old Grandad sixteen-ouncer instead. The real hero was the conservation officer who caught him hunting without a fishing license."

"Well, whatever the reason," Hudson said softly, "I appreciate what you did. It took guts. You were willing to take the guff for my mistakes without a complaint. John R.," he said even more softly with his eyes cast downward into the bay, "I know I ride you about not having any goals or the courage to stick with them. You've shown me you have more grit, more—I don't know . . . But I'm sorry. Maybe I forget that you're seventeen years old at times. Someday you'll figure out what you want to do, and now I'm sure you'll achieve it. I may get off the road before too long, and we might be able to work things out together."

"Off the road? How?"

"Two investors have shown an interest in the tape series. One is Jay Edwards. I thought maybe you knew."

John R. was surprised and said so. He felt worse than ever about the jewelry box, not to mention the necklace. Time was working against him with each day's delay in the return of the merchandise.

Impulsively John R. blurted, "Speaking of Mr. Edwards, wait until you see what he sold me on credit." Diving into the engine hold, John R. reemerged with a green garbage bag.

"I hope he didn't charge you too much. The general store sells them for $1.79," joked Hudson.

John R. was breathing with difficulty as he unfolded the bag, then the oilskin. He held the mahogany box in his hands with arms outstretched for Hudson to see.

"That's nice, John R.," Hudson stated without any enthusiasm. "Who's it for? Do you have a girlfriend?"

"For Mom. Mr. Edwards gave me the box. He threw it in when I bought this." He opened the box quickly so that the necklace which was lying against the dark red velvet sparkled in the fading light of the setting sun.

Hudson whistled as he picked up the necklace. "He sold you this on credit? It'll take you twenty years to pay it off."

"Not really. He sold it to me wholesale. It was a demonstrator model."

"A demonstrator model? What's that?" ·

"A display model, I mean. It was in his showcase for a long time, and he couldn't sell it, so he wholesaled it to me."

"How much did you pay for it?"

"$25 per month," John R. answered too quickly. He was beginning to sweat and fidget. He bounced around from one leg to another as if dancing on hot coals.

"The interest alone must be greater than that."

"Nope . . . Interest free . . . No interest . . . Nope, that's right . . . No interest on this one . . . Uh-uh."

"Well, I'll have to thank Mr. Edwards for his kindness. What was the total bill?"

"It was $2,000, but you can't say anything to him about it. He's a very private person, and I wasn't supposed to say anything to anyone about this. He likes me, but he's afraid his regular customers will get mad if this deal leaks out. Don't say anything to him, Dad, please." There was a plea in John R.'s voice which sounded desperate.

"All right, I won't say a word. This still doesn't add up to me. It will take you over six years to pay him off. That's not a good use of his money. Perhaps I should pay him off, then you can pay me back."

"No!" shouted John R. "You can't. That is, I don't want your help. I mean, this is my business. You have told me for so long how I never had a goal to work toward, and that was true. So when Mom became a grandmother I decided I wanted to do something really nice for her. Mr. Edwards listened to my problem one day, and before too long we had a deal. But to make this work I've got to pay for the necklace on my own. I appreciate your offer, but this is my idea, my problem. It's mine."

"John R., that is really good."

"It's not bad, is it?" John R. breathed a soft sigh of relief. "It's starting to get chilly out here. Can we head home?"

"Not yet, buddy." Hudson stared straight at John R. "I just want you to know that I'm proud of you." With this, Hudson wrapped his arms around John R. and hugged him until tears came to the young man's eyes.

TWENTY-FOUR

Kelly and John R. each received a thank you note attached to a small package. Both notes read, "A small reminder of the big help you were to me when I needed it," signed by Jay Edwards. John R.'s package contained a gold signet ring with the initials JRH engraved in a sweeping cursive script. Kelly was given a delicate gold-chain bracelet which she wore daily. John R. never wore his ring.

"So was your father impressed?" Kelly asked with a twisted grin.

"I'd say so," John R. answered without enthusiasm.

"Boy, you seem real pleased about it."

"I'm not sure if he was buying it or not. He's a lot of things, but he's not dumb. I just want to get the necklace and box back as soon as possible. How do we do that without being caught?"

"First, we don't rush. Next, we devise a plan which covers all the angles. This includes making up a cover story as to why your mother won't get the necklace after all. We don't want your father coming down on you again now that he's impressed."

Kelly pulled sandwiches out of a wicker basket and handed one to John R. Seated in the village park next to the marina, they developed a variety of ways to return the goods. Kelly wanted to take the necklace with her the next time Mrs. Edwards called for a hair appointment and slip it into the drawer at an appropriate moment. John R. didn't accept this idea; he said it was his problem now, not Kelly's.

No amount of figuring led them to a clear, simple solution. A skin rash on John R.'s stomach visibly displayed the internal apprehension he was feeling about a quick return of the merchandise. Kelly was patient, continually stressing the need to wait for the right opportunity. Neither seemed bothered about anybody or anything around them. Their preoccupation with the necklace and the jewelry box absorbed all their attention.

One of the people they didn't observe was a round-faced man who stood behind a large elm tree across from the park's entrance. Despite the warmth of the summer sun, the stranger wore a tan raincoat buttoned right up to the collar. He held a *Sports Illustrated* in front of him, but it was obvious he was not reading the magazine. Instead, frequent shifty glances were cast at John R. and Kelly as they held their discussion at a redwood picnic table.

When it appeared the pair had finished lunch, the stranger threw the magazine into a garbage can, stuffed his hands into the pockets of his raincoat, and walked straight toward the table where the pair was seated. The legs of his pants were cut three inches too short, allowing his white socks to flash as he took short, choppy steps. When he reached John R. and Kelly, he stood at the head of the table without saying a word. John R. thought he was a friend of Kelly's, and she thought the stranger knew John R. All three looked at each other as if they expected a conversation to begin by someone else. John R. broke the impasse by asking if he could help the stranger.

"Ever hear the name Swinford before?" the man growled.

Neither John R. nor Kelly had.

"You'll be hearing it a lot. That's me . . . Lester Swinford. Ever hear the name Edwards before?"

John R. and Kelly nodded their heads yes.

"I've been hired by Edwards to look into a matter of a missing piece of jewelry from his house. You two don't know anything about that, I suppose?"

"What are you talking about?" Kelly shot back quickly so John R.'s look of panic wouldn't be picked up by the stranger.

"It seems some jewelry has disappeared from Mr. Edwards's house. He hired me to find where it might be located. Lester Swinford is well-known for this type of investigation."

"Are you a cop?" inquired Kelly.

"Private investigator," answered Swinford. He took out a crumpled card which looked like it had been printed by a hand stamp and passed it to Kelly. After looking at it carefully, she passed it to John R.

"How do *we* figure into this, Mr. Swinford?" Kelly asked with an edge to her voice which John R. had not heard before.

"The two of you are on a list of people who have visited the Edwardses' house in the past month." Swinford flipped open a small spiral-bound notebook as he spoke. "Matter of fact, you both have been in there in the last couple of weeks."

"So?" Kelly answered coolly.

"So did you see anyone or anything that looked suspicious near the house?"

John R. finally spoke. "I just play tennis out there. The only thing that looks suspicious is my backhand." He tried a smile, but Kelly shot him an icy stare to keep him quiet.

Swinford repeated, "Suspicious backhand" and wrote something in his notebook.

"That was supposed to be a little tennis humor," John R. protested. "I'm always joking around."

"Well, I'm not," said Swinford seriously. "Not much humor in theft."

"I think John R. was trying to say we didn't notice anyone who looked suspicious. Of course, there was a boat which was anchored off the shore for several days. That's unusual at The Pointe, and the boat hasn't been back since."

"Boat?" asked Swinford as he swung open his notebook.

Kelly detailed how a sailboat had been spotted about one hundred yards from the Edwardses' beach. It was an unusual spot to anchor even though a dinghy was tied to the transom, because there was nowhere to land on The Pointe since outsiders were kept away by the private security patrol. Swinford scribbled furiously as Kelly expanded her story, which finished with an observation that the boat was gone the day John R. and she took Edwards to the hospital.

"Any unusual markings on the boat?" Swinford asked. "Did you get the license number? What color was the boat?"

Kelly told him it was a white boat with no unusual details. Although she didn't get the identification numbers, she did notice that a man and woman on board had been on the deck sunbathing naked.

"No kidding?" John R. remarked innocently.

Swinford was taking notes as fast as he could, flipping pages as he went.

"Oh, and one other thing, Mr. Swinford . . ."

"Ma'am?"

"I think I remember the name of the boat. It was the *Daffy Duck*."

"This is good," said Swinford.

"I'll say," John R. muttered to himself.

Swinford stayed for several more questions, his notebook jammed with scribblings. To Kelly's surprise he asked for his card back. "Be on the lookout for that boat," he said to John R. "You workin' in the marina and all, it might come in for service."

"How will I get ahold of you if I see it?" John R. questioned as he played along with the mythical boat story.

"Don't worry, I'll be around. And if you see them, look out. They're probably slicker than snot on a doorknob." He turned on his heel and walked away in short, choppy penguin steps, his white socks flashing as he walked.

After Swinford was out of sight, John R. moaned, "Boy, are we in trouble now."

"What trouble?" replied Kelly. "That jerk is no problem."

"A private investigator is no problem?" John R. whined. "And what was that story about a sailboat and naked sunbathers?"

"He bought it, didn't he?" she answered. "Look, that guy is a clown. He asked us the license number of the boat and if it had any unusual markings. Did he think boats have tattoos and license plates? He'll be driving to every marina within a hundred miles of here looking for a sailboat named *Daffy Duck* manned by a naked crew."

"Kelly, we've got to get the stuff back to Edwards fast."

"No hurry, no hurry. This Swinford jerk may be following us for a day or two. We don't want to do anything unusual."

"I'm getting worried," he said with concern. "My father might get wise. Swinford might get wise. I could be taking a criminal justice lab next semester without going back to college."

Kelly sat on his lap and played with his hair. "Sweetie, you and I are in this together. We've already proven that we can't be hit by stray bullets." She kissed him on the cheek and played with his hair again. Within seconds thoughts of a stolen necklace were not what was on his mind.

"He's good, I tell you."

"He's a jerk," she argued. "How many people wear a raincoat in the middle of summer?"

"He's like Columbo," John R. answered. "It's part of an act. He's supposed to look silly, but it's because he's working on an idea. I think he knows."

Kelly could not convince John R. that Swinford was a bumbler because in her own mind she wasn't sure of it herself. The detective's behavior was so obvious that she too began to wonder what he was really thinking. For the past three days he had stood near the park beneath trees or in front of gift-shop windows eating ice cream cones. John R. said he counted five ice cream cones devoured in one afternoon, each one eaten while Swinford wore his tan raincoat, which bore drippings from the ice cream, which couldn't withstand the summer heat as well as Swinford. The little round-faced man had also worn the same black polyester pants and white socks for the past three days, causing John R. and Kelly to wonder if he had any other clothes.

Each day Swinford also walked to the marina gas pumps while John R. was on duty and asked him, "Seen any *Daffy Ducks* today, kid?" The absurdity of it convinced John R. that Swinford was aware of everything and was mocking his and Kelly's attempt at a cover-up.

At the end of the second day, John R. decided to avoid Swinford by taking *Angel Eyes* out for a night cruise. Faking a fishing trip, John R. idled away from the marina. At the edge of a pier, Swinford lapped a chocolate cone, his round beady eyes fixed on the departing Tiara as it escaped his less-than-subtle scrutiny.

John R. went far from Westport and sat until the bay's only illumination came from a thin moon and cottage porch lights miles away. He welcomed the blackness of the night as it provided a shroud for his activity. Pulling back the cover, John R. lowered himself into the engine compartment and returned topside with the oilskin-wrapped jewelry box, which soon made a graceful arc into the lake.

The quiet lapping of the water against the hull of *Angel Eyes* was punctuated by the plunking sound of the box as it floated momentarily on the surface, then sunk silently 320 feet to the bottom of the bay. With outstretched hands toward the sky, John R. lifted the necklace to see it sparkle in the moonlight before sticking it safely in a pocket of his jeans.

He lowered himself into the engine hold again, this time with tools and a flashlight. He unbolted the flexible tube connected to a blower which exhausted gas fumes from the engine compartment. The necklace was stuffed into the tube, which was then reconnected to the blower. Flipping the blower's switch, he smiled as the exhaust system worked smoothly without giving a hint about the gleaming filters which the gases passed by.

"Blow it out your ear, Swinford," John R. said out loud with mock confidence.

TWENTY-FIVE

Dear John R.,

Don't ask me how I know—a mother senses things, but you're either in trouble or in love. Maybe it's all the same (I'm only joking!). I'm not going to stay with your sister that much longer. I could stop by to see you before the summer is out. Are you going back to college?

Your father says you have a surprise for me. I'm afraid to guess what it could be. Nonetheless, I am beginning to understand what Paul means when he writes, "I know both how to be abased and I know how to abound: everywhere and in all things I am instructed to be full and be hungry, both to abound and suffer need. I can do all things through Christ which strengthens me" (Philippians 4:13).

I look forward to seeing you again soon. Whatever is going on you can overcome not because of your own goodness, but because of God's mercy. Trust me—I know this to the depth of my being.

Love,
Mom

John R. panicked, relaxed, then panicked again. What did his mother know? How did she know? Was she talking to Hudson again, and if so what did *he* know? For as long as he could remember, she seemed to be able to read his mind, to sense his every thought. But even from 2,000 miles away?

And what was that business from the Bible? What was she trying to tell him? Was Christ going to give him some kind of strength? If so, how would he ask Jesus for help? Wasn't it all too late anyway?

The summer sun was intense, but he was so preoccupied with his thoughts that the heat didn't phase him. Neither did it appear to bother Lester Swinford, whose ice cream-stained raincoat bumped against John R. as he reread his mother's letter. Looking up, John R. began to say "sorry," but recognizing Swinford said nothing instead.

"Hi, kid," said Swinford unsmilingly. "Seen any *Daffy Ducks* today?"

TWENTY-SIX

Gloria Laurie refused to attend Hudson's seminar, although she agreed to meet him in the motel lounge when he was finished with the lecture. He was both brilliant and awful during that session. The delivery of the material was quick, witty, and fresh-sounding in spite of the fact that it was the 1,242nd time he had given the same talk. Heads bobbed. Participants smiled, laughed, and cried at Hudson and themselves as he told them how to actualize life by learning to invest in themselves. But he failed to hear their questions at the level of their pain. Flippant replies such as "Visualize, visualize!" or "It's in the book" were hollow and shallow. Participants picked up by his slick delivery and his cheerleading enthusiasm were dropped down by his unwillingness to listen to the statements behind the questions he was asked. His preoccupation with Gloria blocked any ability to care beyond himself.

When the lecture was finished, he rushed back to his room to shower and change. Inspecting himself in the mirror, he tried to pretend that the extra weight he was carrying flattered him. The tightness of his belt pinched him back to reality.

The lounge was dimly lit. An empty bandstand with a drum set flanked by eight-foot speakers at both ends of the platform gave an eerie appearance in the glow of the subdued red spotlights. Hudson was grateful for the band's absence as his eyes adjusted to the low light level.

She was seated at a booth near the back of the lounge. Smoke from her cigarette circled upward in a serpentine fashion. Her blonde hair was cut short, and it was more metallic looking than he remembered. Excessive blue eye shadow and heavy makeup could not be subdued by the lounge's faint light. Her face was as he remembered it—a strong jaw which projected toughness softened by pale eyes which seemed more gray than blue. They were like the eyes of a timber wolf he had once seen on a wildlife poster; hungry, haunting eyes which had burned into his memory for over twenty-five years in their penetrating, mysterious way.

"I'm sorry you couldn't come to the seminar tonight," he said, ignoring all attempts at small talk.

"I could have come," she answered. "I chose not to."

"Any particular reason?"

"Well, you sent me your book and I read it. It's full of words like 'authentic' and 'sincere' and 'choice.' So I asked myself, do I sincerely choose to hear the lecture? The authentic answer was no. Sorry."

"Quite all right," he smiled. "Not many people would be that honest. Does that mean you didn't like the book?"

"It's full of words like 'authentic,' 'sincere,' and 'choice.'"

"Which means?"

"Which means little to me," she said flatly. "I'm still into obligation, responsibility, and faking it. As a man you can use the language of your book, but let me tell you there hasn't been a day when I authentically wanted to do the dishes, nor did I ever really choose to clean a toilet bowl. It's just stuff I do because it has to get done."

"I'm afraid we're off to a bad start." Hudson leaned back as she blew a cloud of smoke in his direction.

"Why are we here?" she asked. "I told you on the phone I'm not buying anything."

"And I'm not selling anything."

Her cold gray eyes looked straight into his. "Hudson, why not be authentic right now?"

"O.K.," he responded and took a deep breath. As he was about to speak, a cocktail waitress placed napkins in front of them and took their order.

"Where was I?" he asked.

"Trying to be authentic," she answered.

"Right. Twenty-five years ago you were appearing in a lounge in Cleveland, and I was in the audience that night. Matt Dennis played the piano for you."

"Yes?"

"There was a lot of noise in the room, and while you were singing you looked at me—probably because I was the only one paying attention. It was as if you were singing to me alone."

"Really?"

"Yes. My friends even noticed. I'll admit I was impressed. I sent flowers the next day. I tried to call, but they told me you had gone to Chicago."

"So?"

"So I married the girl I was pinned to, had kids . . . Truthfully I'd think of you now and then, but within the past five years, especially the last one, I couldn't stop thinking about that night."

"And?"

"And I decided that unless I could find you again so we could talk about that night I'd never be able to grow beyond my current level of development."

The waitress returned with their order.

Lifting up her glass of white wine, Gloria said, "Here's to honesty, Hudson."

He clinked his glass against hers. "So I've told you about me. How about you?"

"How about me," she repeated with a tone of sarcasm. "Three cheers for me." She lifted the glass to her mouth and took a long swallow.

"So?"

"So here we sit twenty-five years later. I'm wondering where in the world you came from, and you're wondering where I've been, and neither of us knows where we're going. Life's a mystery, isn't it?" She pulled hard at her drink. Hudson motioned the waitress to bring her another one.

She said, "I have been all over the country, but the last ten years have been spent right back here where I started. You might say I took the long way home."

"Cleveland is your hometown?"

She nodded as the waitress brought more wine. Gloria held a cigarette in her hand, waiting for Hudson to light it, but he didn't smoke and rarely carried matches. He fumbled through his pockets like a video on fast forward, but came up empty. She fished a lighter from her purse, slid it to him, and inhaled deeply as he lit her cigarette.

"What year was it when you were here?"

He felt let down by her question. She obviously did not remember him after all. "1963. The weather was warm for that time of year. The heat was blasting in the club as if it was freezing outside."

"1963. Matt Dennis. The Cherry Tree Lounge."

"That was the place!" Hudson said excitedly, hoping she remembered him too.

"Around that time there was Evanston, Bloomington, Lansing, Chicago, New York, St. Louis, and Madison. There was also Mort Sahl, The Kingston Trio, Shelly Berman, Jerry Vale, Chad Mitchell, and even Tony Bennett."

"I'm not following you," he confessed.

"Late fifties, early sixties I was the opening act for a lot of those shows. Either that or I was in the vocal background. Played a lot of college towns in addition to the big-city clubs. Nobody really comes to see the opening act, but it was good exposure, and it sure beat some of the dives I was working in."

"Then you remember that night in Cleveland?"

She took a drag on her cigarette, then another sip of wine. "Hudson," she said, "I barely remember 1963."

"I know it must seem foolish to you. It's just . . ."

"Just what?"

"Just the way you were looking that night, I guess. Not the

way you looked as much as the way you stared and the impact it has had on me. It has become," he searched for the correct phrase, "an obsession."

Her gray-blue eyes looked into his again. "I really don't remember." Her statement was colder than her eyes, which didn't seem to blink. As an afterthought she added, "Sorry."

After a few moments of embarrassed silence by both, she exhaled in a soft moan and said, "Hudson, I'm going to level with you. I'm not in the habit of opening my soul to people who say they saw me twenty-five years ago, but I think I can trust you."

He signaled the waitress to bring Gloria another drink. He started to speak, but she raised her hand to silence him, took another puff of her cigarette, then snuffed it out.

"Twenty-five years ago I was hot stuff . . . On my way to the big time. My agent had hold of one great property. He sold me as the new Peggy Lee. But a funny thing happened on the way to the top. I wanted it all, and I wanted it now. 1962, '63, somewhere in there I stared using coke."

"Cocaine?"

"Yeah, it existed then too. It wasn't as fashionable then. Marijuana was just making its debut. I have always been ahead of my time. Any rate, by 1963 I was a pretty heavy user. Half the shows I did I did stoned. A technique I developed was to focus on somebody in the audience and concentrate on that one person. When I was high, I'd see everything, hear everything. I was flying. To block it out, I'd lock on somebody just to stay focused. Problem was that when I crashed, I came down hard. Sounds like you were seeing me at a time when I was making a nosedive toward mother earth."

"I had no idea."

"You weren't supposed to. Anyway, by the late sixties drugs were as available as Hershey bars. Speed, LSD, and coke were more prominent than the Holy Trinity. And I paid for worshiping at the wrong shrine." She took another drink, lit another cigarette, and inhaled so deeply that the tip of the cigarette glowed a bright orange. "In less than ten years this 'sure thing' became a 'never will be.' I didn't even make the 'has been' category. One failed marriage and several close calls later, here we sit. Now you're the hot stuff traveling the country and I'm the one in the audience."

Hudson laughed out loud as the cocktail waitress put another glass of wine in front of Gloria. "I am not only not hot stuff, I may be in the 'has been' category you never attained. Believe me, it's not such a great place to be."

"Here's to us then, Hudson," she toasted. "One 'has been' and one 'never will be.' How does the song go? 'Isn't it rich, aren't we a pair?'" She sang the line, but went no further into the song, taking a drink instead.

He raised his glass to her toast. "What is so crazy is that I'm supposed to be an expert on behavior, and I don't understand what kept driving me to you."

"I'll bet I do," she said with a wink.

"No, it's not that. I can't deny that those thoughts crossed my mind, but it was more than a sexual urge that drove me."

"I never said it was sex. It's something more powerful, and sex just gets thrown in sometimes."

"More powerful than sex? What life force is that?"

She inhaled her cigarette again, took a drink of wine, then set the glass down. Leaning forward slightly, her cold eyes began to look glassy. "It was made perfly clear to me by my ex-husbun. Or maybe it was by one of my boy friens. Doesn' matter," she slurred.

"I want to hear this," he said.

"I remember now. Was one of my boyfriens. He was running 'round on me. Funny thing is that I ha' been running round on my husbun', but it didn't help me understand it any better. I asked him why he did it. Wasn' I woman enough for him? Know wha' he said?

"Said it had nothin' to do with me. Said we're all lookin' for the Perfect Person. Thas wha' he called it, the Perfect Person theory. Capital letters on Perfect and Person. Said when times get tough and our wives or husbuns or kids or jobs get to us, we go lookin' for someone, anyone, who represents no pain, no responsibility, no trouble, jus' comfort and acceptance."

"There is no such person," Hudson said.

"A' course there is. There's plenty of 'em. Thas why we go huntin' aroun' on each other. They're all perfect. That is, until you get to meet 'em, talk to 'em, and listen to their troubles, which are gen'rly worse than the ones you heard from the one you're runnin' 'round on."

"So they're not perfect. You're admitting it." Hudson was beginning to lose patience with Gloria's drunken speech. He slid the glass away from her, hoping she wouldn't notice.

"No, you don' get it. They're perfect in your mind. They don' complain, don' sweat, don' bring you any problems. As long as they are kept in your mind and you don' meet 'em, they remain a Perfect Person."

"Then why do we pursue them? Why did your husband . . ."

"Boyfrien'," she corrected.

"Why did your boyfriend run around on you if he knew the perfect always turned out so badly in real life?"

"Simple. We all love to dream. 'Member that song from *South Pacific* that said you got to have a dream? It's true. We hope that there really is a Perfect Person, we dream it, and we make ourselves believe that we've been lyin' to ourselves about reality. The nex' morning, a week later, a month later—or twenty-five years later—we find the dream was all a lie. The Perfect Person doesn't exist, but we call ourselves a liar again and give it another try. Am I makin' any sense to you?"

"I know what you're saying, but I don't know if I can accept it. Thousands of people have read my book or seen my seminars, and they have turned their dreams into reality."

"Know wha' your book does, Hudson? It deceives a reader who knows there really isn't a Perfect Person out there into believing that he's his own Perfect Person. You get people to dream big dreams about themselves since they can't depend on others. Visualize, energize, and that other stuff is a fancy way of saying, 'You are the Perfect Person; don't rely on others to be per-

fect for you, do it yourself.' Truth is, Hudson, we're all pretty
stinking. But we do love to lie, especially to ourselves. Where's my
glass?" she said, looking for the wine. "I feel like I'm sobering up.
That's a dangerous condition for me to be in."

"So what would you recommend that we do? Crawl in a hole
and hope the world goes away?" Hudson was beginning to tire
of her, and he looked at his watch. The band started tuning their
instruments, and before long he knew the lounge would be puls-
ing with loud music and noise. He wanted to be alone, not in the
lounge with Gloria, the band, or anyone else.

"Hudson, if I knew the answer to that one I'd bottle it. You got
trouble with your wife, your kids, your job? Go home and work
'em out as best you can. They may not be perfect, but I'm not
your Perfect Person either."

"No, you're not," he said as he rose to go. "I'm sorry I bothered you, Gloria. I'm afraid I've been a bit of a fool."

"Hudson, don't apologize. From you it doesn' sound authentic
and bein' authentic is importan'. I read that someplace. Besides,
for the past five years I was a Perfect Person. That's about four
years and 364 days longer than my average."

She waved to the waitress to bring more wine as Hudson
slowly walked out of the lounge.

TWENTY-SEVEN

"It's gone!" he shouted in disbelief.

"What?"

"It's gone." This time he whispered. Kelly handed John R. a flashlight, and he swished the beam throughout the engine compartment. He shook the blower tube again, but nothing came out. His hands patted under the engines, around the bilge, and into every opening he could imagine where the necklace might be. Kelly jumped into the compartment beside him, and together they fumbled and searched for the missing jewelry.

"Where's the box?" she whispered.

"I threw it overboard."

"What for?"

"At the time it seemed it would be easier to hide the necklace without the box. I was getting spooked by Swinford."

"Are you sure you took the necklace out?"

"Of course I'm sure. We've had it stolen from us."

"It's not possible!" she gasped. "You must have misplaced it."

"Up the hose of a bilge pipe blower is not misplacing it."

Kelly was nearly hysterical. "Are you sure that's where you put it?"

"How would I forget putting a diamond and emerald necklace up the tube of a bilge blower?" John R. was beginning to catch her hysteria.

"What did you put it up there for anyway?"

"It was a foolproof scheme, that's why. Nobody would look up there."

"Somebody sure did. This is going to mean big trouble, John R. BIG trouble."

"Kelly, just think positive," he said with all the sarcasm he could muster.

"May I board, captain?"

"Dad!" shouted John R. "Why are you here?"

"Because I'm always received so warmly, of course."

John R. put his palms on the floor and popped up from the engine compartment like a giant jack-in-the-box.

"Problems with the engines?" Hudson asked.

"No, no . . . No problems. Preventative maintenance is all."

"John R., would you help me up please?" Kelly asked.

"You remember Kelly?" John R. asked his father as he pulled her from the engine compartment. Together they quickly slid the hatch cover over the opening.

"I don't think I recall . . ." Hudson said lamely.

"We met at your place around Memorial Day," Kelly said softly.

"Do you know how to fix engines?" asked Hudson.

"No . . . John R. was showing me what to look for if anything ever goes wrong."

"He's very handy. He keeps this boat in Bristol condition. Say, why don't the three of us go out to dinner tonight? Boar's Head at 7? My treat. I've got some great news about a project I'm working on. I'd like to test the ideas off you two tonight before I see the investor." Hudson was grinning broadly.

"Sorry, I have an appointment tonight," Kelly answered. "It was kind of you to offer, however. John R., thanks for everything. I'll see you again . . . soon."

She placed one foot on the gunwale of *Angel Eyes*, the other on the marina walkway, and lightly stepped off the boat. Kelly moved past the other boats, trotted through the park, and quickly sped away from the parking lot in her Corvette. She didn't notice the ice cream-stained raincoat of Lester Swinford beneath a huge oak tree less than thirty feet from the route she traveled.

Lester looked at the marina, then watched her as she pulled away. He flipped open the small notebook and noted the license plate number of the car Hudson was driving. Beside it he wrote the number from Kelly's Corvette's plate. He watched her turn the corner, looked toward Hudson, gave a small shake of his head, and walked away with his hands stuffed in the pockets of his raincoat.

Lester Swinford hated to admit it, but he was baffled. Jay Edwards was sure some jewelry was missing, but there was no proof it was stolen. Edwards, like a dummy, kept no inventory of any of the jewelry, furniture, or silverware in the house. Every jerk with a 35mm. camera was smart enough to take pictures of his household goods so the insurance company would have some idea of what a property might be worth in the event it was stolen or lost in a fire. But Edwards apparently relied too much on The Pointe's security guards and fire department to keep him safe. *Maybe that's what happens when you have so much you don't have to worry about counting it any more*, thought Swinford. But if that was the case, how did Edwards know exactly what was missing?

Swinford had stopped at twelve marinas in the area asking for a sailboat named *Daffy Duck*. Fortunately, none of the harbor masters or kids at the marinas laughed at him for asking. Boats all had goofy names; some weren't even in English. By Swinford's estimation, anybody who spent time and money waiting in the middle of a lake for the wind to blow them around in big circles wasn't entirely sensible anyway. He only asked a couple of times about the naked crew part. Sailors were crazy enough as it was, but asking about a nude crew was even more than Swinford could handle.

He chuckled to himself about having convinced Edwards that John R. or Kelly or Hudson had to know how the theft had taken place. The whole gang would be at the Edwardses' home in a couple of days as the fat detective had convinced the jeweler that a confrontation meeting at the scene of the crime might reveal something. Edwards was opposed to it because he wasn't suspicious enough. He said when he went to the hospital the house was left open and anybody could have walked in. While Swinford wasn't expected to solve the crime, Edwards wanted him to prove that the kid had nothing to do with it. *Fat chance*, thought Swinford. Everybody was guilty until proven innocent as far as he was concerned. Edwards's biggest problem was that he liked the kid too much. Lester would never be tripped up by that kind of sentiment. He didn't like the kid one bit. For that matter, he didn't like the father either. And except for her cute little figure, he didn't care much for the hairdresser. When you got right down to it, Edwards himself wasn't much to write home about. Lester figured that even though he himself wasn't softhearted, at least he was fair.

Swinford plotted the strategy for the confrontation meeting. Nothing fancy; just attack one, then the other. Look for an opening, then attack. Spot a weakness, then attack. Eventually one of them would crack. A Lester Swinford crack-attack was on the way. He was ready. He hummed the theme music from *Rocky* to himself. *Rocky Swinford*, he thought. It had a nice ring to it.

TWENTY-EIGHT

The Boar's Head was jammed with patrons dressed in bright-colored clothes. Everyone in the restaurant except Hudson sported a tan ranging in color from bright red to deep bronze. Having spent a summer inside planes, rented cars, and motel rooms, Hudson's complexion had a gray-white pallor which looked completely out of place in this crowd of tanned tourists. Dressed in charcoal gray slacks and a white, button-down, broadcloth shirt, Hudson looked like wallboard in an art gallery when compared to the rest of the diners in the restaurant. John R.'s skin was leather-brown, and his hair had bleached to the color of straw. Because the Boar's Head did not take reservations, Hudson and John R. were forced to wait in an area next to the bar where couples chatted, laughed, and joked with each other. Hudson and John R. said nothing to each other during this time, not because of anger, but because everything they had to say was so important it seemed inappropriate to begin talking until they were seated.

They were led to a booth which provided them the privacy they needed. Hudson grinned expansively as they ordered. He encouraged John R. to have a big meal as this night was going to be a celebration.

"It's obviously good news," John R. began. "I haven't seen you this happy since you won the high school championship for the third time."

"It's about that exciting, maybe better. And you have played a big part in it, I'm sure."

John R. thought to himself that there was very little he had been involved with which could make anyone happy. "Tell me what it is," he said curiously.

"Tomorrow night I'm meeting with Mr. and Mrs. Jay Edwards at their home on The Pointe."

John R. tried to stay calm. "And I had a big part in that?"

"Very big is my guess. Among other things, I find that Jay Edwards likes you very much. He finds you polite, sensitive, and a better tennis player than him. He also told me how you saved him from a bad case of hyperthermia."

"You're not going there to talk about me though, are you?" John R. was exploring as much as he was asking.

"No, not really. We're going to talk about financing the video project. Or more specifically, about Sinbad Enterprises financing it."

"Who's Sinbad?"

"Turns out it is Mrs. Edwards's little hobby horse. Jay Edwards stays with the jewelry business because he understands it. Mrs. Edwards has a series of business ventures she dabbles in that have no connection to the jewelry business. She puts up the venture capital, then sells out when profits are being turned. She apparently has a keen sense of what works and what doesn't."

"That's great, Dad," said John R. "Does that mean you'll be off the road for a while?"

"I think so. It depends on the shooting schedule and how much creativity I can put into the project."

"Creativity?"

"I've thought of a new twist to the seminars which I'd like to put into the series. Up to now the emphasis has been on improving yourself for your own good. What I'd like to do is show people how to invest in themselves so they can help others as well as themselves. Jay Edwards said that's what he really likes about you. You don't take yourself too seriously, and you're willing to help anybody whenever you can."

"There's something you should know, Dad."

"I know."

"You do? How?"

"Edwards tipped me off."

"He knows then?"

"Sure. He spotted it right away."

"He did?"

"Yes, and I don't mind telling you that it's more than a little embarrassing."

"For me too," John R. said in hushed tones.

"Well, don't be. It happens to all of us sooner or later. Edwards said you seemed very preoccupied lately, and he thought there was a girl in your life somewhere. Tonight you were there with Kelly, and all the pieces started to fall into place."

"They have?"

"Of course. I was young once myself. She looks older than you though. I'm just hoping you aren't deciding to do anything rash. We need to talk about your future."

At that point John R. realized that Hudson knew nothing about the stolen (and now missing) jewels. The crowd noise in the busy restaurant did not seem loud enough to drown out the thumping of John R.'s heart. The sense of relief he felt by not being discovered was replaced by the anxiety of knowing that someday the truth could be known to others. In fact John R. had told someone about the deception and had planned to return the necklace whether Kelly liked it or not, only to find it missing.

During dinner Hudson provided an animated description of changes he would make in his seminars by video. The major thrust would focus on improving the lives of others as well as one's own life. As Hudson became more vocal, John R. grew even quieter. Hudson was now so passionate about his concern for others that he failed to notice that his son had not spoken a word other than "uh-huh" and "I see" for over twenty minutes.

Hudson finally slowed down as the waitress cleared their empty dishes. "So tell me about the projects in your life. Anything I should know?" he asked John R.

John R. looked away. "Kind of," he said softly.

"Kind of good or kind of bad?" Hudson asked curiously.

"Kind of both actually." John R. tried to sound more confident, but a crack in his voice betrayed him.

"Your girlfriend's not in trouble, is she?" Hudson was speaking softly now.

"Kind of," John R. replied.

"Kind of? She can't be 'kind of.' She either is or isn't. There is no 'kind of.'"

"You mean pregnant? No, it's not that kind of trouble. It's a different trouble, kind of."

Hudson leaned across the table and said as patiently as he could, "John R., I'm not very good at guessing games, but if you give me a couple of clues other than the words 'kind of' I may be able to figure this conversation out."

"I don't think this is the time or the place, Dad."

"Let's try. Do it in charades if you like. Go ahead. How many words does it have?"

"It's a necklace," said John R.

"That's not how charades work," joked Hudson. "You give me signals, and I say the words."

"It's not too funny, Dad. Remember the necklace I showed you that I got for Mom?"

"Yes. It was a beauty."

"It wasn't for Mom."

"Oh, oh. I think I'm getting closer. It was for your girlfriend, right?"

"Not exactly."

"Not exactly?"

"Not exactly."

"We've switched from 'kind of' to 'not exactly' for clues. Am I getting any closer to knowing what happened?" Hudson looked bewildered.

"Not exactly."

"O.K., John R., let's try charades again. For whom did you buy the necklace? Give me a signal here. How many words in the answer?"

John R. held up one finger.

"One word. O.K. How many syllables?"

John R. held up one finger.

"One word, one syllable. O.K., we're on a roll. Now, who did you get the necklace for?"

John R. pointed at Hudson.

"O.K., let's see. Father? No, that has two syllables. Hudson? No, same thing. Man? That has one. Good grief, John R., you bought a necklace for a man?" Hudson sounded genuinely shocked.

"No, I did it for you," said John R. softly.

"For me? What are you talking about? I don't even wear a gold chain like half the fruitcakes in this country are doing. Why would I want a diamond and emerald necklace?"

"I didn't say you wanted one. I said I did it for you." John R. was speaking more loudly now to hide the trembling he felt in his throat. "You were always on my case about not having any goals, no motivation. So I decided—that is, *we* decided to borrow a necklace and jewelry box from Mr. Edwards. The plan was that I'd show you, you'd be impressed, and shortly after that we'd put it all back."

"Oh my."

"We no more than took the stuff and my stomach told me it was all wrong. It started out so harmlessly. You were impressed, and then I actually believed for a while that it might work out."

Hudson exhaled deeply, looked around the crowded restaurant, leaned toward John R., and in a soft, confident voice said, "All right, son, we've got to make this right."

Hudson's mind was racing, although outwardly he appeared calm and unflustered. It was the same technique he'd used as a coach when games were close. On the inside his mind and stomach churned options and alternatives, while on the outside he seemed relaxed and unbothered. One local sportswriter even commented that Tom Landry and Chris Evert looked like nervous wrecks compared to H. J. Hudson on the sidelines. Now he was debating how much to tell Edwards and what impact it might have on Sinbad Enterprises. No clear plan emerged, so he continued to talk to John R.

"We've got to get the necklace back to Edwards without damaging your relationship with him." Hudson hoped the real motive of keeping his own relationship with Edwards untarnished was not obvious to John R. "We could send it back in an unmarked package."

John R. shook his head.

"Or we could have it returned by a neighbor, or have it turn up mysteriously at the Village Hall delivered by a woman who thought Mrs. Edwards lost it at a party."

John R. shook his head again.

"Or we could tell him the truth, which I take it is what you're suggesting by constantly rejecting every idea so far. I guess you're right, although I'm not ready to deal with the mechanics of that meeting yet."

"That won't work either, Dad."

"John R.," Hudson said while gritting his teeth, "I am trying as best I can to hold my temper. Can you give me one good reason why not one of my ideas will work?"

"Because the necklace is gone."

"Gone?" Hudson's face could not disguise his confusion. "Gone where?"

"Gone. I don't know where. It's gone is all."

Hudson repeated, "Gone . . . gone?"

"Gone, gone," agreed John R. who began to giggle with a nervous energy. "That tickles me. We sound like a clock that just struck 4. Gone-gone-gone-gone."

"John R., you're up to your eyeballs in trouble and you're making jokes. Doesn't that strike you . . ."

With the words "strike you" Hudson also began to giggle. Then it turned into an outright laugh, although he didn't know why. Together they howled, said "gone-gone-gone-gone" again, and continued laughing despite the smiling confusion of the diners at the nearby tables.

"C'mon, Cisco, let's went," laughed Hudson.

"We be gone," responded John R., and they laughed all the way out of the restaurant.

TWENTY-NINE

They walked past the closed art galleries and curiosity shops along the streets of the village without saying a word to each other. On one occasion Hudson began to snicker, which touched off John R. again. Hudson finished the job by saying, "gone-gone-gone-gone" in his best Westminster chimes imitation, causing both to laugh until their sides ached and they had to sit on a park bench to catch their breath.

Fog was creeping across the peninsula with a silent determination. The bay in the distance was dark and quiet. The fog appeared to swallow boats which were slowly trolling near the marina, so that only their lights could be seen as they motored along. The silence was punctuated by distant laughter or the indiscernible shouts of sailing crews who were giving commands to helmsmen who were having difficulty finding the mouth of the port.

"I really love it here," said Hudson with genuine sincerity.

"Me too . . . Except for the mess I've made of things."

"We do have trouble, son."

"Not *we*. It was my doing, not yours. I never figured it would get so far out of control."

"Give me the whole story, John R. I don't want you to hold back."

As they sat on the park bench watching red, green, and white lights mysteriously pass each other in the distance, John R.

unfolded the entire episode, including the unusual behavior of
Lester Swinford. When John R. finished the story, a roar of laughter from a party boat on the bay echoed throughout the marina
area.

"Glad somebody thinks it's funny," said John R.

"Does anyone else know about this?" asked Hudson.

"Besides Kelly? Yeah, one other person . . . kind of."

"No more 'kind ofs' please. Who else?"

"A pastor in town."

"How would he . . ."

"I told him."

"Everything?"

"No . . . Just that I was troubled and wanted to know what
Jesus would say in my situation."

"And what did the pastor say?"

"He didn't say much at first, but he asked a lot of questions.
Finally he said that Jesus came to save us and that rather than tell
me what Jesus would say, I could talk to Him myself."

"Did he give you a toll-free number?" asked Hudson bitterly.

"In a way, yes. He told me how I could turn my troubles over
to the Lord and pray for His guidance."

"Have you done that?"

"Yes."

"And?"

"There's only one solution. I've got to face Mr. Edwards and
tell him what happened. I don't know how I'll pay him back. If
he wants to press criminal charges . . ."

"I don't think he'll do that. If we talk and I agree to cover the
losses, I'm sure he'll drop any idea of prosecution. Besides, it's
only a couple of thousand, which sounds like a lot, but I'm sure
he finances bigger amounts for people he likes."

"It's more than two thousand."

"How much more?"

"Somewhere between eight and ninety-eight."

"Eight and ninety-eight what?"

"Thousand."

"Somewhere between eight and ninety-eight thousand *more* than the original two? Nah . . . You're kidding!"

"I'm not. Kelly said the necklace was worth at least five figures, maybe six."

"Well, which is it?" Hudson asked with agitation. "Five figures or six? You can feed the nation of Ethiopia for a year on the difference between the two."

"I don't know. I'm no expert on jewels, and I wasn't about to get it appraised."

Hudson began to pace in front of the park bench. The façade of calm, controlled emotions was breaking down with each step he took. Thoughts raced through his head, but no plans, no solutions, no contingency actions came to him. His hands began to shake. For the first time in his adult life, he was without an alternative that would allow him to slip the grip of a difficult situation. Nothing came to him except emotions; fear, confusion, and despair were first, then anger.

"Why did you go to a preacher at all?" he shot at John R.

"I've been getting these letters from Mom . . ."

"Telling you to see a preacher to help you find a lost necklace?"

". . . and she's changed," John R. continued. "She's stronger, more honest, more assured."

"If she knew what I know, she'd blow a gasket. How do we keep this from her? She could barely handle changing to Daylight Savings Time each summer. This will overload her circuit breakers forever."

"She's tougher than you think. She's become a Christian . . ."

"And they're tough? A bunch of Bible-bangers who plan Sunday school picnics every July and building programs every time the church needs a new coat of paint?"

"She doesn't say that much about churches. She mentions God and Christ and how certain Bible verses have made her understand things better. I wanted to know if God could work that way in my life too."

"Well, buddy, I don't think there's a Bible verse for a missing necklace worth five or six figures. That means I've got to reach down to my old bootstraps and pull up one more time." Hudson seemed very tired.

"The pastor said God was capable of miracles even today if we just believe."

"That might work for the preacher, but I'm from a different seminary. The Right Reverend Bust N. Hustle was the dean of my school, and he said if you need a helping hand in life, look at the end of your arm."

"But you wrote in your book, 'A person is capable of believing only what he can visualize as the truth.' I can see God at work in Mom's life and mine. Doesn't that mean we should believe He has the answers?"

"If it works for you, yes. I just don't see it that way," said Hudson quietly. "I just don't see it at all. It's me against the world. That's the way it has always been, that's the way it will always be. Life is the fourth quarter of a championship game with the score tied and no time-outs left. What I wouldn't give to have the referee blow a whistle now so I can catch my breath." He sat down heavily on the park bench and stared vacantly into the fog.

THIRTY

When they parted, Hudson invited John R. to stay at the house again. John R. wanted to accept, as the time spent together in the restaurant was the best conversation the pair had in years. His father had been willing to listen, to act as a partner, to laugh. But outside the restaurant John R. felt the strain between them resurface, although he felt no bitterness towards Hudson. John R. knew he had added more burden to their lives at a time when an additional problem would have to fight its way into a crowd of others. He was disappointed in himself for what he had done and for the way he had described his new life in Christ. While he had a sense of strength and security which he had never known before, he felt inadequate at expressing himself in a way his father could understand. Instead, he talked about his mother's letters, which were meaningful to John R. but confusing to Hudson, who had not read them and couldn't understand how she had changed.

John R. turned down the invitation to sleep at the house that night because he said the fog would drive many boats into the marina and he wanted to be at work very early to attend to all the extra traffic. He agreed to return to the house the next night, however. While it was true that the marina would be overloaded with boats rafting off each other in twos and threes, John R.'s real motive was to spend time alone in prayer, and he knew his father could not understand that need. They parted with an agreement to get together at the end of John R.'s shift to discuss the best way to explain everything to Jay Edwards.

By the time John R. had reached *Angel Eyes*, the fog had covered the entire peninsula like a large circus tent which had collapsed. Visibility was limited to inches, making sound the best method to indicate distance and location. Boats trying to find refuge in the harbor blew horns while their nervous crews shouted, so that anyone in earshot could take evasive action. Crews already tied down for the night laughed, shouted, played music, and sang to celebrate their good fortune and to reassure themselves that they were really alive even though no one could see them.

John R. volunteered to help the attendants on duty by directing incoming traffic to slip spaces where there was a chance to raft off other boats. After three hours of frantic activity, he dragged himself to *Angel Eyes*. The marina was quieting down, and he was grateful for the chance to unwind. He sat on a bench seat in the stern, bowed his head, and prayed in earnest for God's guidance the following day. John R. committed himself to God's will whatever the consequences.

"So talk to me," said a voice near him.

"Who's that?" he asked as his heart raced.

"Who were you expecting?" asked the voice.

"Is that you?" he said in amazement.

"Why do you sound so shocked? I thought we were friends." Kelly flashed a beam of light at him from the galley. She directed the flashlight into his face, and he winced as she walked closer to him.

"It didn't sound like you," he said defensively.

"I disguised my voice to scare you," she said. "This fog makes it spooky out here, doesn't it? Were you surprised?"

"No, I was . . . Yes," he admitted. "I was surprised . . . a little."

She sat next to him and switched off the flashlight. "John R.," she began softly, "we've got to figure out what we're going to do about the necklace."

"I'm done thinking, Kelly," he said. "It's gone . . . simple as that. I've got to take the consequences."

"No!" she shouted. "We've got to try to solve this. There's got to be an explanation, kid."

He said, "No explanation. They're gone-gone-gone-gone. Sounds like a clock striking 4, doesn't it? Gone-gone-gone-gone."

Kelly stared at him impassively.

"Maybe you had to be there," he said flatly.

"Look, kid," she stated, "you've got a great sense of humor, but I didn't come here to listen to impersonations of Big Ben. We've got bigger matters to handle."

"Kelly, it's no use. It's gone. I've thought of everything, believe me."

"Think some more." Her voice sounded menacing. He had known the tone she used to give orders, but this was stronger, threatening.

"Somewhere in this world there is a necklace that closely resembles these." The beam from her flashlight illuminated a pair of emerald and diamond earrings in the palm of her left hand.

"Where did you get . . ."

"Same place I got the necklace," she answered. "That's why we've got to find the necklace . . . Can't break up the set."

"What's going on?" John R. questioned. "This doesn't make sense anymore."

"That's how we feel," she answered.

"We?"

"*Oui* . . . We, *monsieur*," she said as she aimed the flashlight at a figure sitting on the pier post next to *Angel Eyes*. The fog made it impossible to discern any features, but it was clear that a man with folded arms was listening to the conversation.

"Who's that?" gasped John R.

"Names aren't important, but you know each other. Now, let's talk about the necklace."

"What's to talk about? I don't know any more than you do. Now, what's going on?" He sprang to his feet, leaped up on the pier, and faced the man who had been sitting on the post. John R. was inches taller, but was outweighed by at least sixty pounds.

"This is, this is . . ."

"My estranged husband?" she responded.

"Right."

"Wrong. I don't have a husband. Never been married as a matter of fact."

John R. argued, "This is the guy in the pickup truck."

"He is. Meet Sonny Granelias. Sonny is everything I told you except he's not my husband. He's also meaner than what I've said about him."

Sonny smirked, spun John R. around, and pushed him back into the boat.

"John R., Sonny and I have come to the conclusion that since you and I were the only ones who knew about the necklace—and since I don't have it—you decided to do something cute with it." Kelly was cold, direct.

John R. felt Sonny's warm breath on the back of his neck. "That's baloney. What would I do with it anyway?"

"Same as we would do—find a buyer and sell it."

"You were going to sell it? We agreed to return it to Mr. Edwards."

"Nice idea, kid," she said. "Very noble, but nobility doesn't pay the rent. Now, you'd better tell us where you stashed the necklace or Sonny may get mad."

John R. felt Sonny move behind him. "I thought I shot this guy," John R. mused.

"Not even close," she chuckled. "The gun had blanks. Sounded real though, didn't they?"

"What about the time on the boat when . . ."

She interrupted, "This is going nowhere. Better tell us where it is. Sonny's getting anxious."

"Why are you doing this, Kelly?" John R.'s voice couldn't hide his confusion and pain.

"Why? Why is the dumbest question anybody can ask, kid. Who really knows why anything. People who can answer why are generally covering themselves after they've already made up their minds."

"Tell me how you made up your mind then."

"Years ago I knew I had to get out of here. People like you come up in the summer, live in places that we can't afford as year-round houses, and call them your summer homes or cottages or even cabins.

You've grabbed up all the prime land so that we can't even afford property any longer. Next come your toys—boats, bikes, motorcycles. We get to clean them, service them. We've become a village of domestic servants and hamburger flippers. Everybody loves the bay, the scenery, the summer months. But who's around when the cherry-shakers are breaking their backs from dawn 'til midnight? Who's here when the snow is four feet deep and everyone hopes they've stacked enough wood to last the winter? Not you summer gypsies who have moved back to places that must really be something if these are your summer homes. At least the fudgies are honest. They come here looking stupid, acting stupid, and then leave with a little less money in their pockets. Nobody up here wants to be like them. But people like you and The Pointe types dangle a whole way of life in front of us that is something we'll never see except as outsiders in our own territory. Well, that's life, I thought. That is, until the day I read your father's book. Why can't I have what you've got, I thought. Why not visualize something sweet for Kelly beyond cutting hair and sniffing the stink of permanents? Why not use the people who use us as a way out of this place? Why is a dumb question, kid, but why not is a good one."

"Boy, have I been a jerk," said John R. softly.

"It's genetic, kid," she chided. "It's caused by the X-Y chromosome." She knew John R. would understand the remark even though Sonny wouldn't. "Now it's your turn to get honest. Sonny has a trick he likes to do. He holds people by their feet, then dunks them underwater. It softens even the hardest head."

With this, Sonny slapped the back of John R.'s head, propelling him forward to the gunwale. John R. spun around angrily, only to have Sonny's left hand slap him across the mouth so hard that John R. tasted blood.

"I told you he was mean," Kelly taunted.

"Is this a private party or can I join too?"

John R. recognized Hudson's voice. "Dad!" he shouted. "Boy am I glad to see you."

Still standing on the pier, Hudson answered, "That's a cut above my greetings as of late. This fog is so thick, I don't know who all is down there."

"Kelly is here again. She brought along her pet ape. Oh, sorry, Sonny, it's so foggy I couldn't tell it was you."

"Kelly, how convenient. I must confess I've been doing a little thinking about you tonight. We need to talk," said Hudson strongly.

"Now ain't this cozy?" Another voice on the walkway of the pier caused them to squint toward a large beacon of light which was being flashed in their direction. "We're all together, savin' me the trouble of findin' each one separately." John R. recognized the voice of Lester Swinford, who jumped onto the boat. The reflection from the beam of light revealed the same raincoat Lester had been wearing for weeks.

"I'm here to bring you all an invitation. That is, almost all. Who is this?" asked Swinford as he swaggered toward Sonny.

"He's nobody," said John R.

"Well sir, everybody except Mr. Nobody is invited to Mr. and Mrs. Edwards's house tomorrow night at 8:00 o'clock P.M. Dress is casual, but be on time."

"What for?" asked Kelly sharply.

"'Cause Mr. Edwards don't like it when people are late."

"I mean, why should we go there?" she said impatiently.

"We're going to have a little talk—all of us. That is, everybody except Mr. Nobody. He ain't invited."

"I was supposed to meet Edwards tomorrow to discuss a business transaction," said Hudson.

"And I had something I had to tell him," echoed John R.

"We'll probably get around to it," replied the little round detective who spit tobacco juice toward the water. Most of the wad landed on the gunwale of *Angel Eyes* and dribbled down the side of the boat.

"What if I don't want to come there?" Kelly asked defiantly.

"You want to be there," answered Swinford in the same tone she used. "It's either a nice chat at The Pointe tomorrow night or a not so nice chat at the police station later. Get my drift?"

Swinford let out a loud grunt and stretched back onto the walkway. He looked back into the boat and said, "See you all tomorrow. By the way, the guard at the gate has all your names, so you're cleared to go through. That is, everybody except Mr. Nobody. Of course, he ain't invited anyhow."

THIRTY-ONE

John R. and Hudson rode together silently and arrived ten minutes early. Kelly pulled Sonny's pickup truck into the concrete semi-circle drive at exactly 8 o'clock. Swinford met each person at the door as they arrived at the Edwardses'. He ushered them into the den, where the stereo played a nearly inaudible Montovanni tape. John R. and Kelly sneaked glances at each other, their eyes darting away when contact was made. By contrast Hudson stared hard at the beautician, his eyes fixed on every move she made.

"Drinks anyone?" asked Edwards cheerily as he entered the room a few minutes later. "Forgive me for not being here to greet you. We're opening a new store in Boca Raton, and there are some problems with a leasing agreement."

Edwards wore a white linen sport coat, raspberry shirt, white sailcloth pants, socks which were color-coordinated with his shirt, and a pair of tasseled loafers. Although everyone except Swinford declined anything to drink, Edwards insisted on going to the kitchen for a tray of soft drinks, fruit juices, white wine, and a beer for Swinford, who drank it straight from the bottle. For the first time John R. could remember, the rotund little detective did not wear his raincoat. Instead he was dressed in black slacks three inches too short, which exposed his familiar white socks. A short-sleeved knit sport shirt which could not stretch over Lester's girth gapped wide from his belt line, exposing a black hairy stomach each time he tilted his head to gulp from his beer.

Edwards was casual and cheery, making references to the weather and the need to lose more weight as he took a chair by the desk. John R. and Hudson sat on the love seat, while Kelly squirmed in one of the leather wing chairs. Swinford stood in the doorway, shifting his beady eyes from one person to another. He took another gulp of beer, then belched.

"Lester," said Edwards politely, "perhaps you should begin this discussion."

"Keerecht." The little fat man stepped toward Edwards, pulled the last slug from the bottle, belched again, then placed the empty on top of the desk once owned by James Madison. As Swinford returned to the doorway, Edwards relocated the bottle to the tartan carpet.

"Well, sir," he began, "this is just about the strangest case I've ever been on. The folks in this room did send me on one merry chase."

"Mr. Edwards, may I say something?" asked John R.

"Later, John R. Let's allow Mr. Swinford to proceed." Edwards spoke as quietly and politely as always to his young friend.

"Thank you," said Swinford, except the way he said it it sounded like "Think you."

"Think about what?" asked John R.

"Huh?" grunted Swinford.

"You said, 'Think you.'" John R. wasn't trying to be cute, but Swinford misread the remark.

"O.K., let's start with you, wise guy." Swinford tugged on his sport shirt to pull it over his stomach, only to have it rise halfway up his back.

"Watch your mouth, Swinford. That's my son you're speaking to." Hudson spoke in a low growl, but the intensity in his eyes was loud and bold.

"Well now, listen to this, the wandering father has spoken. Let me set the stage for you so you don't jump on your high horse too often."

Swinford began to pace in front of Hudson, John R., and Kelly in his choppy penguin steps, his white socks flashing beneath his short-legged trousers. "First a necklace and earrings were missing from this household." When Swinford said "earrings" John R. shot a glance toward Kelly. "Later it was discovered that a jewelry box like those Mr. Edwards gives away to certain clientele was also missing. Turns out the necklace and earrings aren't registered, recorded, or even photographed. Turns out the jewelry box is numbered, and a record of each one given away is noted—who received the box, what date it was given, any inscriptions on the brass plate, and, most important, what was in the box when it was given away. Don't that beat all, Mr. Hudson? Jewelry lies around this place like loose change, while a lousy jewelry box has a history as long as Kunta Kintay. Remember him? The black feller from the 'Roots' TV show."

"What's your point?" asked Hudson.

"What's my point? What's my point?" The little fat man slapped himself on the forehead, arched his back, and flashed a hairy navel in Hudson's face. "My point is that we can trace the approximate date the box was stolen by the record of the box given away before it. Now do you understand?" Swinford bent over at the waist so that he was face to face with Hudson.

"And?"

"And you, Mr. Hudson, were in this area during that period of time. You played golf here at the invite of a new resident who didn't have you approved by whatever committee they have to check out guest golfers. Obviously you had access to the homes in The Pointe. With your business failing like it is, it would be easy for you to drive here, walk in like one of the residents, and leave with a few baubles which could help your financial troubles." Swinford stood and stared at Hudson, who was enraged at the allegation but outwardly showed no signs of distress.

"That's ridiculous," scoffed Hudson.

"Of course it's ridiculous! That's why this little scenario is better." Swinford hand-signaled Edwards to fetch him another bottle of beer. "How's this sound"—he belched—"in terms of possibilities, that is? Cute little Miss Kelly here has been out to this house

on several occasions to fix Mrs. Edwards's hair. One day she gets
the idea to lift some jewelry to help pay for that fancy car she
drives. The two of you cook up a deal where she tells you where
the stuff is hidden. Between the two of you a deal is cut, and she
calls you when Mrs. Edwards is under the hair dryer and Mr.
Edwards is gone. That way you can walk right in because Kelly
has the Mrs. captured with curlers and a comb. Besides, the Mrs.
has an ear problem and wouldn't hear you as long as the dryer
was blowing."

"Stupid!" spat Kelly.

"Ludicrous!" Hudson agreed.

"Of course it's stupid and licorice or whatever that fancy word
is. That's why this next little scenario is better yet. All three of you
plan a little scheme to baffle even the cleverest of minds. Mr.
Hudson, you tell Junior here to help you out of your money jam
by keeping Edwards busy. You also enlist the help of Miss Kelly
over there since she has access too. To your delight, Mr. Edwards
conks out one day playing tennis with Junior. You ain't even in
town at the time, but Junior alertly runs upstairs, pockets the
gems, then pulls a really clever stunt. He calls Miss Kelly and has
her bring an ambulance and a doctor. While they're loading Mr.
Edwards's body into the ambulance, Junior slips Miss Kelly the
jewels, and off they go in the ambulance to split the proceeds with
you at a later time."

"Preposterous!" shouted Hudson.

"That's bizarre!" Kelly agreed.

"Of course it's prosperous and brassiere or whatever."

"That's not how it happened," said John R. in a soft, gentle
monotone.

"Of course that ain't how it happened!" snapped Swinford. "I
gotta admit all kinds of plans went through my head. First one
of you did it, then the other, then a pair, then all three. This case
really was a mind-bender. And you two really had me going with
that naked crew aboard the *Daffy Duck*."

He began to smile, took another gulp of beer, then belched
again. "For a while I figured you were playing a game with me.

Come to find out it was a true story. Musta been some sight," he said as he winked at John R.

"Lester, it didn't happen that way," repeated John R. more forcefully.

"I know it didn't happen that way, Junior. What do you think I am, some kind of fool? It didn't happen that way or any other way because it never happened!" Saying this, Swinford opened a drawer in the James Madison desk and extracted the emerald and diamond necklace in question—the very same necklace taken previously by Kelly and John R.

"Now, don't that beat all?" laughed Swinford. "I've been working this case for weeks and weeks, chasing my butt all over this county lookin' for a crew of naked sailors aboard a *Daffy Duck*. I've staked out around the clock watching either Junior or Miss Kelly or the wandering father here. I musta ate two dozen chili dogs and twelve dozen ice cream cones on this job. People told me how great it was up here. What bull! This is a lousy part of the country. Why, you can't even get a decent meal around here. There's not one single McDonald's or even a lousy Arby's in the whole county. It ain't even civilized for cryin' out loud. I think I ruined my stomach!"

"I think we're losing the point," said Edwards quietly to Swinford.

"Well, at least you know you've lost something," snickered Swinford. "That's better than you did with these little trinkets." Lester dangled the necklace between his fingers. "Why would anybody pay good money for somethin' as foolish as this anyway?"

"It's a mystery even to me," replied Edwards.

"Well, you've done pretty good tryin' to figure it out," answered Swinford as he rolled his eyes around the contents of the house.

"I think we're losing the point again," persisted Edwards.

"The point is," Swinford began while shifting his gaze from John R. to Kelly to Hudson, "I've been thinkin' one or more of you lifted the stones. Come to find out you didn't because they never were taken. Mrs. Edwards misplaced them. Put 'em in a spare purse instead of her jewelry drawer. Boy, it must be nice to have so much you can't remember where you put it."

Swinford chugged the rest of his beer and put the empty on the James Madison desk.

"Thank you, Lester, you may go now."

"Can I take a beer with me?"

"Help yourself to anything in the refrigerator."

Swinford penguin-stepped his way out of the den toward the kitchen. Edwards rose from the desk chair, walked to the sliding door of the den, and slammed it shut with a loud bang.

"I wonder if the three of you would mind staying for just a few more minutes," he said. "I have some unfinished business I'd like to complete here tonight."

THIRTY-TWO

Edwards stared at Kelly, Hudson, and John R., who blushed as soon as eye contact was made. The jeweler took a deep breath, then exhaled in a long, nearly inaudible sigh. As he adjusted his shirt collar and buttoned his sport coat, Edwards said, "I must apologize for Lester. He is a complete boor, I know. If there is any excuse I can offer, it is that Lester is a living example of the well-worn statement that we can choose our friends, but we inherit our relatives."

"You're related?" gasped Hudson.

"My wife's second cousin," nodded Edwards. "I'm pleased that you were surprised."

"That's a distant relative," Hudson replied.

"Not distant enough, I'm afraid. Lester is a victim of a plant closing in Tennessee, and his benefits have expired."

"I thought he was a detective," John R. said quizzically.

"Oh, he is. He was right when he said this was his strangest case. That's because it's his only case so far. Against my advice, my wife thought we could help Lester financially by hiring him, which would allow him to preserve his dignity. Based on what I've seen, Lester has precious little dignity that needs protection."

"Mr. Edwards, may I say something?" asked John R. Kelly glared at him as he spoke.

"Indulge me for a bit longer," answered the jeweler. "I promise I'll listen to you shortly."

"It's getting late, and I've got to be going," said Kelly as she stood to leave.

"You'll stay!" There was an edge to Edwards's command that was as hard and sharp as the diamonds he sold. As if to correct himself, he added pleasantly, "Please be seated, Kelly. We won't be much longer."

Edwards brushed the sleeves of his sport coat, then walked to his desk to relocate the beer bottle left by Swinford. He unbuttoned his coat and stuck a hand in each pants pocket. Hudson, John R., and Kelly all looked at him with anticipation. Instead of speaking, he stood silently for a long period of time. In the background Montovanni played the score from *Camelot* through twin tower speakers.

"Lester," mused Edwards to no one in particular. "Lester, Lester, poor Lester. I'm not sure whether to pity him or laugh at him. Which would you choose, Hudson?"

"If he's a relative of yours, then I pity you."

"That's kind of you, but it begs the question. What's to become of him? He really does believe that this was never taken," said Edwards as he lifted the necklace with his left hand. "Of course, those of us in this room do know they were taken, don't we?"

Silence was the only response to his question. Montovanni was doing a violin version of "Those Seven Deadly Virtues" in the background.

"Don't we?" he repeated with a hardness.

"Yes."

"Uh-huh."

"Mmm-hmm."

"Fine. Knowing Lester as you do, I think you'll understand my decision to hire a slightly more qualified detective to trace this trinket. In a relatively short period of time he had suspicions about how it was done. We had all but given up on even locating the necklace. However, persistence on his part plus meticulous attention to details such as extra maintenance being done aboard *Angel Eyes*—a boat which is rarely in need of so much attention—led him to make a search which was quite illegal but very revealing. What is so curious is that somehow the necklace managed to fall into a bilge blower tube. Even more puzzling is that a matching pair of earrings didn't fall into the same tube. Would any one of you care to explain that to me?"

Hudson looked at John R., who looked at Kelly, who looked straight ahead. Her face appeared cold and emotionless, but she could not control a small twitch on the right corner of her mouth.

"Perhaps this will aid our memories. The earrings look like these." Edwards walked to the James Madison desk, opened a drawer, and lifted a pair of diamond and emerald earrings on an open palm, elevating them like a stage magician.

"How did you . . .? You broke into . . .? When . . .?" Kelly shot the questions at him.

As if he hadn't heard her, Edwards continued, "The missing earrings go with this necklace." With his right hand he lifted the jewelry given to him by Lester Swinford.

"By contrast, these earrings are paired with this item . . ." Bending down to the open drawer in the desk, Edwards extracted a second necklace exactly like the one he held in his right hand. Extending both arms in front of him, Edwards displayed twin necklaces whose design and sparkle announced their arrival with a dazzling fanfare.

"Two of them!" John R. exclaimed.

"They're exactly alike," mused Hudson.

Kelly's eyes darted around the room. The twitch on the corner of her mouth was keeping time to Montovanni's version of "If Ever I Should Leave You."

"Lovely, don't you think?" Edwards slowly paraded around the room holding the necklaces as if he were holding imaginary babies in his hands.

"Identical twins," said John R.

"Beautiful," said Hudson.

Kelly said nothing, but her mouth twitched faster.

"One of you is correct, the other is not as accurate," answered Edwards. "Both necklaces share the same design, the same settings, and the exact same number of jewels."

"But the quality of stones is better in one than in the other," Hudson guessed.

"In a manner of speaking, yes," agreed Edwards. He held up his left hand. "This necklace has very clear diamonds and emeralds with several inclusions. By contrast, the stones in this necklace are clearer and the emeralds have fewer inclusions."

As he lifted his right hand closer to his eyes, he grimaced. "The problem is that these stones are cubic zirconia and imitation emeralds, making the piece quite inconsequential in value." As he passed by Kelly, Edwards dropped the necklace in her lap. The twitch on the corner of her mouth had stopped, and her jaw hung open.

Hudson said what the others thought. "You're saying the missing necklace was a fake?"

"Obviously not a fake," chided Edwards. "The necklace is quite real. It just does not have the same value."

"You hired a detective to find it though," countered Hudson.

"Two detectives actually," corrected Edwards. "And I would love to know where the earrings are."

"Are they valuable?" asked John R. cautiously.

The jeweler shook his head. "Worthless."

"Mr. Edwards," John R. said seriously, "I'm a college dropout. Could I play back what I think you've said?"

"Confused, my young friend?" smiled Edwards.

"Lost," John R. agreed.

"If you think you could help me recover the earrings, I may be willing to clear this up for all of us."

Hudson, Kelly, and John R. looked at each other, unsure of what to say. Kelly's twitch had been replaced with a hard, tight-lipped glare. "Police?" she said strongly.

Edwards dropped his chin, raised his eyebrows, opened his eyes very wide, and said, "Dear Kelly, if I had wanted the police involved, I wouldn't have hired a private investigator, would I?"

"Two of them actually," John R. added.

Edwards nodded in agreement.

"If the cops aren't called in, you'll get the earrings," Kelly agreed softly.

Although Edwards heard every word, he made Kelly repeat the statement again, only more loudly. When she was done, he said, "Please, let's all get comfortable. I have a story to tell which requires that we relax. May I get anyone something to drink or eat first? *Mia casa est tua casa*, you know."

In the background, Montovanni played the finale to *Camelot*.

THIRTY-THREE

He led them from the den to the kitchen with its black-and-white marble floor. Despite their protests and denials of not being hungry, Edwards insisted on putting a plate of sliced fruit, cheese, and crackers on the table. Glasses filled with ice were placed on the kitchen counter along with a wide array of fruit juices and soft drinks.

Edwards directed his guests to the cane-bottomed chairs edged around a large oak table. From above, the ceiling fan circled so slowly it gave the impression it would go still at any moment. Hudson and John R. were quiet, but looked considerably more at ease than Kelly whose tight lips and glaring eyes could be read as either fear or anger. By contrast, Edwards flashed a wide smile at his guests as he folded his hands together, fingers intertwined, then placed his forearms on the kitchen table.

"Anything else I can get you before we begin?" he inquired. All three shook their heads no, although Kelly's movement was barely discernible.

"I'd like to tell you a fairy tale. Do you like fairy tales?" All three didn't know how to respond, but it didn't matter because Edwards plowed ahead without waiting for their responses.

"Once upon a time," he began, "there was a young man who worked in a drugstore." He looked at them apologetically and said, "This doesn't sound too much like a fairy tale so far, but most of the fairy tales with kings, queens, princesses, and dragons have been overexposed, so I'll give this one a twentieth-century tone. Where was I?" he asked absent-mindedly.

"In a drugstore," John R. answered.

"Yes . . . Thank you, John R. The young man did numerous chores at the store, including working behind the soda fountain. A lost art in today's world, I'm afraid. While behind the counter one day, a beautiful princess entered the store. While she was not in distress in the strictest sense of the word, she did need something to drink. The young man was smitten by her beauty on the spot, and since there was no dragon to slay, he did the next best thing under the circumstances—he mixed her a cherry Coke. On the house, of course.

"The damsel was very grateful for his kind act, so she repeated the whole scene again every day for a week to see if it was a fluke on his part or could he really mix a cherry Coke with some degree of consistency. He did so well that she invited him to her castle for a visit.

"This is where the story sounds like the usual kind of fairy tale stuff. The damsel wasn't a true princess in terms of having a king and queen as parents. In this particular story she had parents who thought they were a king and queen because they lived in a castle. Actually the castle was one of four owned by the king and queen. The other three were in California, France, and northern Michigan. The princess and the young man continued to see each other at places other than the drugstore since she was convinced in her own mind that he had the cherry Coke routine down pretty well.

"As young couples will do even in twentieth-century fairy tales, they fell in love. This made the couple quite happy. Love seems to have that effect on everyone whether they're in a fairy tale or not. But the king and queen were very unhappy about this love affair, proving that you can't win 'em all even in a fairy tale.

"'Mixing a cherry Coke is no talent,' said the queen. 'No future in them either. Bottles are the future for America,' the king roared. He said this with real conviction because his plants produced bottle caps. He was right, of course. Soda fountains were on their way out; bottle caps were in.

"But that wasn't the real reason the king and queen opposed the love interest of their daughter. While they would never come out directly and say so, the reason they opposed the romance was because the young man was Jewish.

"Remember, I told you this was a twentieth-century fairy tale. In a way you can understand the dilemma this posed for the king and queen. After all, there are no Jews in the usual fairy tales, so they didn't have any examples of what to do. Mainly they talked about soda fountains, cherry Cokes, and how there was no future for the young man and the princess.

"So the young man and the princess were heartbroken, but determined to find a way to consummate their love. One day a jewelry store next to the drugstore went up for sale. Unbeknownst to the king and queen, the princess loaned some of her dowry to the young man, who got a special deal on the business for two good reasons. First, the original owner needed a quick sale, and, lest we forget, the young man was Jewish. At least that's how the first jewelry store owner saw it.

"Soon the young man was doing very well due in large measure to the fact that the princess sent many of her friends to the young man's store for special bargains. I mean, most of them lived in castles too, but they went there because they knew a bargain when they saw one.

"Two years after the original rebuff, the young man and the princess approached the king and queen on the subject of marriage. 'Oh my!' gasped the queen. 'Bottle caps!' roared the king.

"Despite her royal upbringing, the princess decided to elope with the young man. This just about destroyed the king and queen. It also had a strong impact on the princess, as this was her only major act of defiance in twenty-two years. Princesses are taught to have manners regardless of the issue, and marriage is not the best place to practice one's defying skills."

Edwards pushed away from the oak table; his face turned dark and brooding. He paced around the table in slow, measured steps. The pace of his conversation also slowed, so that the tone of his voice became deeper and almost foreboding. "Years later the princess and the young man would find that they could never have children. The king and queen would remind the princess that it was God's punishment for failing to obey her parents as the Commandments state. Eventually the princess would come to believe this herself, despite the advice of all the wizards who were consulted by the princess on the subject. The princess would become withdrawn, fearing God's wrath forever, continually blaming herself for all the evil which she and the young man encountered while failing to notice how they had been blessed in so many ways."

He paused by the kitchen sink, placed both hands on the counter, and stared out the window into the dark bay which quietly splashed tiny moonlit waves on the shore like diamonds being rolled on a carpet of black velvet. He wheeled around quickly. Hudson, Kelly, and John R. had been staring at him, unsure of what to say or do. When he turned, the somber countenance was gone, replaced by a smile which was more mysterious than pleasant.

"Well, I'm afraid I've digressed," he mused. Without asking he snapped open soft-drink bottles and poured the contents into the ice-filled glasses on the counter. He set a glass in front of each person at the table, lifted his own, and said, "*L'chaim.*"

"Where was I?" he asked.

"The princess couldn't have children," said John R.

"Yes, yes, but before then."

"The princess and the young man eloped," answered John R. again.

"Quite right. Such a helpful young man." Edwards turned to Hudson. "You're quite lucky to have such a fine son."

Hudson nodded.

Edwards returned to the fairy tale in the more musical tone with which he began. "So the king and queen, fearing what other castle-dwellers would think, struck a bargain with the young couple. If they would leave the area, the king and queen would plunder the treasury so that the young man and the princess could begin a business in some faraway kingdom.

"The princess thought it was a heck of a deal and they should

go for it. But the young man was stiff-necked and proud. He preferred to stay and tough it out. Nonetheless, the princess won out,
and the young couple took the money and moved elsewhere. She
parlayed the money by wise investments and became a venture
capitalist. Meantime, the young man continued in the jewelry
business and prospered in his own right. Between the two of them
they had all the material possessions a young couple could want.
They only lacked children and the respect of the king and queen,
who wouldn't visit the couple, but permitted visitation from the
princess on state occasions.

"One day the king and queen appeared at the residence of the
young couple, who weren't so young anymore. It seemed an
enemy kingdom had waged war with a most devious weapon
which reeked havoc throughout the land. The weapon was snap-
tabs. Snap-tabs were devastating the country where bottle caps
once reigned supreme. The treasury, although not in permanent
danger of destruction, had been dealt a serious blow by this insid-
ious instrument of terror. Consequently, the king and queen were
selling off some of their castles, including the favorite of the
princess in northern Michigan. The princess couldn't bear the
thought of seeing that castle disappear, as she had too many fond
memories associated with it. So the not-so-young couple got a
special deal on the castle for two good reasons. First, they had
cash on hand, and, lest we forget, the princess's husband was
Jewish. At least that's how the king saw it."

Edwards paused momentarily, sipped from his cold drink,
popped a green grape in his mouth, then continued, "But there
was one small detail attached to the castle. It seems there was a
covenant connected to the property such that no one in the association surrounding the castle would ever sell to Jews, blacks,
Catholics, or other less-desirable creatures who roamed the earth.
Both the princess and her husband had to agree not to hang the
Star of David from the castle's garage peak. Likewise, bacon,
ham, and spareribs had to be served at every barbecue lest the
lords and ladies in the association ever got wind of the husband's
distorted ancestry. Are you getting the picture?"

"I believe so," answered Hudson. "Were the lords and ladies in the association sufficiently fooled?"

"For a period of time, yes. But one day a black knight entered the association. He had heard from a friend of a friend that the couple was doing charitable acts such as sending ice cream daily to the county orphans' home to disguise the husband's mideastern heritage, which was unwelcome in the land."

"It's true then," said a wide-eyed John R. "Somebody really does it, and it's you!"

"I'm sorry, John R., I don't know what you mean. This is merely a fairy tale, remember?" Edwards paused, grinned his mysterious smile, then continued, "It was even rumored that the husband shortened his given name of Jacob to a more suitable name for acceptance within the association. While none of the black knight's charges were validated, people throughout the land began to retreat from the couple. Getting a bridge game was very difficult. Golf was even tougher. Tennis seemed a possibility since it took only one other player. Even this became a problem as the black knight's rumor swept through the area.

"Enter a white knight in the form of a young man who didn't care about a person's pedigree or where they lived or what they did."

John R. blushed as Edwards spoke. He was both humbled and humiliated because he had in fact disliked Pointe people with the same lack of sensitivity as that described by Edwards.

"The white knight became a friend to the man and in true white knight tradition even saved the man's life at one point."

John R.'s face had turned ashen. "I'm so ashamed," he said out loud.

"Shut up!" Kelly snarled.

Edwards faked surprise with wide eyes. "Such emotion from you two. Remember, this is only a fairy tale."

Kelly's face reddened. "Let's cut the games, Edwards. What do you want?"

Undaunted he answered, "Merely to finish my story."

"Sure, sure," she snapped back. "You'll play around for a

while, and then Swinford will walk in here with a cop to make the arrest."

Wide-eyed, he grinned. "I've never heard of someone being arrested for telling a fairy tale. I didn't think I was doing that bad a job. Mind if I continue?"

"Have fun," she grunted.

"I forgot where I was."

Hudson helped this time. "The white knight saved the man's life."

"Of course. When the princess returned to the castle, she informed him that they had trouble. Some of her jewels were missing."

"Real jewels?" asked Hudson.

"No . . . simulated jewels."

"Where was the danger then?" asked a confused Hudson.

"While the lords and ladies in the association did not care to socialize with the couple, they had no objection to doing business with them. Bargains have no prejudice, it seems. Despite the fine protection given to the castle, the couple decided it was wiser to keep a mixture of real and simulated jewels in the castle. By chance, only simulated jewels were taken, which was curious. It was also an indication that the thief in question was not a seasoned professional. At any rate, when the princess went to dinners, parties, or special occasions, she wore a mixture of real and simulated jewels to attract attention and stimulate interest. When prospective buyers came to the castle they were shown all merchandise, simulated and real."

"Oh, I think I'm beginning to understand," said Hudson cautiously. "As a way to get back at the lords and ladies who snubbed them, the couple showed and sold simulated merchandise as if it were the real thing."

"Never! Absolutely not! Unthinkable! Should a buyer choose a simulated piece, he or she would be told it was already sold or promised to someone else. However, a similarly designed item could be created with the buyer becoming a partner in the creation. In this way the lords and ladies got a bargain, plus they could exercise their artistic talents. You'd be surprised how dread-fully void of artistic talents lords and ladies can be."

"Then where was the danger to the couple if simulated jewels were missing?" Hudson did the asking, but his question was on the minds of the other two as well.

"Ah, that is where the black knight did his most serious dam-age. Should the simulated jewels be discovered by the local sher-iff, he could disclose their minimal value to the newspaper. The lords and ladies who had done business with the husband or the princess would claim they were cheated, even though appraisals would verify their good fortune. The biggest damage, however, would be in the form of derisive remarks, jokes, and statements that would make sport of the heritage of the princess's husband."

"Would that trouble him?"

"Not him, for he's grown to live with it. He also has learned to cry all the way to the bank. The princess, however, would be wounded emotionally. While she visited the castle during the summers of her youth, she was unaware of how contaminated the land surrounding the castle really was. Families who were friends of the king and queen barely acknowledge the princess now because of what the black knight has done. If the sheriff found the missing jewels and made a public disclosure . . . well, let's just say the princess would be wounded, which would grieve her husband who loves her very much. You see, what is so crazy in this fairy tale is that the husband of the princess thought that when you become rich, you had achieved a form of greatness in this country. What he didn't comprehend was that in a land of lords and ladies, kings, queens, and castles, nearly everyone is rich. The only true currency that matters to them is information—good or bad. But I must tell you that bad information is much more valuable. It is sought after and traded with more vigor than any gold or silver."

"So why shouldn't people like us who know the story tell it around the village?" asked Kelly. The hardness in her voice was still present, although she was becoming more curious about the fairy tale.

"This is just a fairy tale, Kelly," he reminded her. "The husband in the fairy tale is quite certain that little will be told because he hired a private investigator—actually he hired two of them—to find the jewels. The investigator who found them knows where they were found and is fairly confident he knows how it was done. What the investigator doesn't know is that the necklace he found is of simulated jewels. Should a certain story be spread around town, that investigator could be called back to testify what he had found. There could even be a real necklace somewhere which I think the detective would identify as the very one he located. In the meantime, the husband of the princess believes there is a pair of earrings that should be returned to the castle's treasury box. It would be a good-will gesture that everyone will keep his part of the bargain. Besides, this fairy tale needs a happy ending, don't you think?"

Kelly nodded at him, "They'll be at the front gate tomorrow morning."

Edwards acted as if he hadn't heard her. "Well, that's about all there is to the fairy tale." He sighed. He rose from the table as if to indicate they should leave.

"Mr. Edwards, any chance of tennis again soon? Summer's nearly over, and I've got to be going back to school." John R. hoped for one more opportunity to visit as he had done before.

"I'm afraid not, John R. I doubt that I'll see you again before you leave here, so my best wishes for a good year at school." Edwards shook John R.'s hand, but failed to notice the pained expression in the young man's face. Edwards turned to Hudson. "I'd like to see you in the den alone for a few minutes if you have the time." There was a tone in his voice suggesting his statement was as much a demand as a request.

THIRTY-FOUR

Hudson followed Edwards from the kitchen to the den, where the jeweler pointed him to a seat on the sofa. Edwards slowly closed the door behind him, slipped off his sport coat, and placed it delicately on the chair next to the James Madison desk. When he turned toward Hudson, Edwards encountered the same wide grin and energetic face which began every "Invest in Yourself" seminar.

"Mr. Edwards, I just want to . . ."

Edwards held up his hand to indicate that he did not want Hudson to continue. "Mr. Hudson, I think you should know that you are very fortunate."

"Yes sir, I am in many ways."

"You have a wonderful son whom I have come to admire this summer. We have had many great tennis games out here, and he has always conducted himself like a true gentleman."

"Thank you. I appreciate hearing that. As you know, I spend a good deal of time on the road, and it's not always easy to be know how he conducts himself. We haven't had the best communication process between us, so it is encouraging to know that he is behaving."

"I'm afraid you didn't understand what I said. When John R. and I were playing tennis he conducted himself like a true gentleman. I won't press you to find out how much you know about this situation, but your son is in a good deal of trouble. The fairy

tale which I told in the other room was a veiled attempt at the
truth. Quite honestly, I would be relieved if many of the rumors
about me could be confirmed publicly. The paradox of bigotry is
that it makes heroes out of some and cowards out of most. I feel
guilty every time I hear the story of James Medgar Evers or
Martin Luther King and I continue to remain silent and secluded.
They could not disguise their race, so they became leaders against
racism. I can conceal myself, however, and in so doing I betray
my own heritage at the same time that I confront my own cow-
ardice. I rationalize that I keep my silence out of love for my wife
whose health is not good, but . . . Out of respect for your son I
have decided to overlook an incident that could be damaging to
him for many years."

With a deep sigh of relief Hudson replied, "I want to thank
you for forgiving my son. I'm sure he has learned a lesson he will
never forget."

Edwards walked back and forth for several moments. He
stopped, cocked his head, and stared quizzically at Hudson. "I
have been debating with myself whether to tell you what I am
thinking."

"Please, I would welcome hearing your thoughts."

Edwards smiled the mysterious grin which disclosed so little.
"I was thinking that it is little wonder that you and your son have
a communication problem as you have not heard a word I have
said so far. I told you that I was willing to overlook an indiscre-
tion on his part, and you thanked me for forgiving him. Let me
assure you that I have not forgiven your son and in all probability
I never will. Forgiveness, Mr. Hudson, is not within me. For too
long I endured many adversities which I couldn't understand.
Some were based upon my religion, which is a farce as I have not
been a practicing Jew for decades. Sometimes it was clear that I
had not gone to the correct college or university. This too I found
a farce. By a good deal of work I managed to finish a college
degree and develop a business which has provided me with a
comfortable living. In spite of that, I found myself shunned by
wealthy sons and daughters whose only evidence of a college edu-

cation is found on the sweatshirts and massive college rings they wear.

"I told myself not to be troubled by such silliness, and I forgave them time after time. Chronic high blood pressure plus a number of doctor and psychiatric visits revealed to me that I had not forgiven them at all. I was acting out a charade. Over time I came to the conclusion that true forgiveness is beyond the bounds of human capacity. My life became much simpler once I arrived at that realization. Hating in return is a much easier process, you see. It was easier on my blood pressure and my wallet. Hating also takes considerably less energy than forgiveness. I found it quite useful.

"Unfortunately, your son does pose a problem for me. I must admit that I really do like him. He has brought me many moments of joy. I was hoping that he was also benefiting from our relationship, but I allowed myself to be deceived."

"Mr. Edwards, if I may speak on John R.'s behalf, I believe he has been made a victim by a young woman who did a number on him that makes Eve's trick in the Garden look like a kindergarten show-and-tell."

"But, my dear Mr. Hudson," countered Edwards, allowing his voice to rise slightly, "I have read your book. John R. was not deceived. He chose his behavior. You argue quite eloquently that we cannot blame others for our mistakes. Rather, we must learn to 'own' our behavior through the choices we make. Are you suggesting your premise holds to everyone but your son?"

"No, but . . ."

"Forgive me for interrupting, but you also say in your book that a person should listen for the word *but* because that is where the real sentence begins."

"You have done your homework quite well."

"And perhaps you haven't," said Edwards so softly that Hudson did not hear the words, yet understood the tone. "Mr. Hudson, let me clarify myself. John R. caused a great deal of confusion in my life. Not because of the missing jewelry, but because just when I found that I was not compelled to forgive anyone, he entered my life. If ever I wanted to forgive someone, it would be John R., believe me." The jeweler looked out onto the lake. The night and the bay were black. Even the moon which had bounced light off the water had retreated behind blankets of cloud cover. "It would just be easier for me if he never came back here again. I'll ask you to honor that wish."

"If that's what you want, of course."

"It is," said Edwards to the window in front of him.

"I'm very sorry. I'll be leaving now if we are through."

"But we aren't quite through yet. I believe you had an appointment with my wife this evening."

"Yes, well, I'm sure that any business transaction we might have had is fallen by the wayside now."

"To the contrary. My wife is not home this evening due to her plane being grounded in Chicago. She wanted to meet you tonight and has every intention of meeting with you early next week to discuss the production of your project."

"But I assumed . . . that is, I . . ." stammered Hudson.

"Let's be clear with each other, Mr. Hudson. My wife knows nothing of the details of the missing jewelry. She is quite relieved that no damage has been done. If she had asked me, I would have told her that I thought your book was pure garbage and didn't merit any further attention. But she didn't ask me, and she never will. Nor for that matter will I interfere with the project in any way, even though I am totally against it. My wife, you see, has the uncanny ability to see business opportunities and potentials that the average person like me can easily overlook. Once upon a time she even saw the potential in a Jewish soda jerk who ended up living in a castle, if not happily ever after."

THIRTY-FIVE

A stunned H. J. Hudson walked to his car, where John R. sat impassively in the passenger seat staring straight ahead through the windshield. Hudson started the engine and said nothing except his name to the guard at the association's front gate.

After they pulled onto the roadway, a raccoon scampered across the road within range of the high beams. Hudson was accelerating so slowly he didn't need to take his foot from the gas pedal to avoid hitting the masked creature. Within another mile a female deer froze in the beams of the headlights. This time Hudson coasted the car to a slow stop. The deer was mesmerized by the lights and stared directly at the car. Hudson was fascinated by the doe's color, a gentle tan which matched her delicate disposition. She was a small animal, only slightly taller than a pony, but fragile-looking with broom-handle front legs. Her ears pointed upward, and she sniffed the wind with anticipation. What John R. and Hudson both noticed were her eyes—large, brown, and unblinking. If she was fearful or angered by the intrusion into what had been her private world, her eyes gave no indication of it. They stared into the car's lights with a look of peace and childlike innocence. She neither advanced nor retreated. Although appearing motionless, her body gave the impression of muscular tension ready to spring like the drawn cord of a long bow.

"I think that's what angels' eyes will look like," whispered John R.

"I hope so," Hudson whispered back.

Moments of silence passed before a car came at them from the opposite direction. The deer flicked her ears and tail, and with two quick trampoline-like bounces on hooves which never seemed to touch the ground she retreated into the woods.

They continued to drive in silence. John R. wanted to apologize, but didn't know how to begin. He decided to determine what mood his father was in so the apology could be tempered in the best manner.

"Did you and Mr. Edwards have a nice talk?"

"Nice," Hudson nodded.

"Think I should see him tomorrow?"

"No."

"Is he mad?"

"Yes."

"Did you talk to Mrs. Edwards?"

"No."

"I loused up the deal, huh?"

"No."

"I'm really sorry, I . . . no?"

"No," said Hudson who laughed slightly and shook his head as the car pulled into the marina. "Noooo," he laughed more loudly as he jumped out of the car.

"You mean the video thing is still on?"

"Yes," said Hudson with both fists raised in the air like a triumphant boxer. "Yes, yes, yes!" He banged his palms up and down on the hood of the car to the beat of the chorus from the waltz "Shall We Dance?" In perfect three-quarter time Hudson sang, "He said yes." Bang-bang-bang! "He said yes, and he said there will be more." Bang-bang-bang! Euphoria swept over Hudson as he waltzed-banged his way around the car's roof, fenders, and trunk, ending with, "With a clear understanding that these kind of things can happen, he said yes, he said yes, he said yes!" Bang-bang-bang!

"Dad, are you O.K.?" John R. was afraid his father had gone on a stress overload. Hudson hadn't been so giddy since winning the state championship for the third time.

"No, I'm not O.K., m' boy," he answered in a W. C. Fields voice, "I'm beside myself." He switched to a Groucho Marx imitation complete with twitching eyebrows and the flicking of an imaginary cigar. "And anybody who is beside myself isn't worth joining."

"Holy cow, you mean you're not mad?"

In a Bela Lugosi voice Hudson answered, "Mad? Mad? Uff course I'm mad. I vant to bite your neck."

"Medic, medic," cried John R. pretending to run away. "There's a sick man over here."

"*Au contrair*, I've never felt better. Have you ever seen a sick man do this?" Hudson jumped from the bumper to the hood to the roof of his car. He beat his chest vigorously with both fists and gave a loud Tarzan yell, "Aheehaheehaaheeaaa."

"Dad, you'd better come down from there. People will think you're a kid, and then you'll be in real trouble."

Boaters from the marina were coming out onto the walkways to see who was making the noise. Hudson saw the crowd he was drawing, and instead of retreating he waved wildly at the onlookers. "Hi, folks. Wonderful evening, isn't it?" His comments drove the curiosity-seekers back to their boats, almost as if they were ashamed of investigating the commotion.

Hudson looked down at John R. "They act as if they've never seen a man on a car roof before."

"They're mad because their cars don't have the lunatic-on-the-roof option that this one has."

"Lunatic? Do you know the derivation of that word?" Hudson eased down to the hood, then the front bumper, and stood next to John R. "It came from the word *luna*, which is Latin for moon. So a lunatic is . . ."

"Latin for a crazy man who stands on car roofs doing Tarzan yells," answered John R. smartly.

"Close enough." Hudson put his arm around John R.'s shoulder. "Look up there," he said pointing at the sky. "The moon is out in full splendor, shining with all its might."

"The moon doesn't shine, it reflects."

"Who cares?" asked Hudson.

"It's an admission question for the Lunatics of America Club. If you answer it wrong, you can't stand on car roofs for a whole month."

"I've got an idea. Let's take the boat out for a night cruise."

"No way. Not in the shape you're in."

"I'll jump on the car roof again," threatened Hudson.

"O.K., O.K., we'll go. Boy, I can hardly wait to grow up so I can act like a kid," John R. grumbled good-naturedly.

THIRTY-SIX

The cloud cover had disappeared so that the white light of the moon illuminated the bay with clear visibility. They were further aided by house lights on both sides of the bay which dotted the shoreline in a patch-quilt pattern of yellows and whites. When Hudson shut down the engines of *Angel Eyes*, the water acted as a sound reflector, so that they were able to hear the laughter of fishermen in small boats as far as a mile away.

"This is about where we stopped the last time we were out together," said John R.

"At that time you told me you dropped out of college. Earlier this evening I heard you say you were going back."

John R. teased, "For seventeen years you haven't listened to me. Tonight you pick out one sentence like you're a contestant in a Mr. Good Ears contest."

"It's important to me. You must have found a goal to work toward. Tell me about it. I'm all ears." Hudson cupped his hands behind his ears and pushed them forward. From the distance he heard a fisherman yelp with delight over a strike.

"Tell me about Mr. Edwards first. Did he give you a million dollars or something?"

"Better than that."

"He liked your book then?"

"Thinks it's pure garbage."

"But he likes the video project idea."

"Totally against it," Hudson said candidly.

"So it's off?"

"It's on."

"Boy, I'm glad I'm going back to college. These adult conversations are tough on a kid."

"Mrs. Edwards is the money behind the deal. She knows little or nothing about the details of the missing necklace. She also happens to be a shrewd investor and sees potential in this venture."

"Dad, that's great. Will you be able to get off the road for a while?"

Hudson became animated. "Yeah, off the road. No more poorly lit conference rooms in overpriced motels. I'm going to be able to create, to think, to visualize a whole new approach." He gazed out onto the moonlit bay. The quiet slapping of the waves licking against the hull of *Angel Eyes* were the only sounds he could hear. Impulsively he shouted, "I love it here."

From a fisherman came a return shout, "Me too, except for all the noise."

"Maybe we'd better go beneath," Hudson said with an impish grin. "It seems I'm disturbing the peace. Besides, I'm hungry. Do you have anything to eat in the galley?"

"Some peanut butter."

"Is that all?"

"A couple of cold slices of pizza in the refrigerator."

"Anything else?"

"I think there's a couple packages of chocolate HoHos."

"I don't think I'm that hungry," grimaced Hudson. "Got any coffee?"

"Never drink the stuff," John R. said as he wrinkled his nose. "It's bad for your health."

They went below to the galley nonetheless and split the one remaining bottle of Pepsi which was aboard. John R. also found an opened box of Triscuits which they shared. The intensity of the moonlight was so bright that it was necessary to switch on only one small light in order to see each other clearly.

John R. took a gulp of his pop, swallowed too quickly, and burped. "Excuse me," he said.

"You must have been taking lessons from Lester Swinford," Hudson laughed.

"So tell me what Mr. Edwards had to say." John R. had a touch of impatience in his voice.

"Actually you heard most of the conversation. Afterward he admitted that he really enjoyed your company this summer."

"So why can't I go out there and talk to him?"

"He made me promise you wouldn't show up again."

"I guess I don't blame him. It's just that I would like to tell him how really sorry I am and ask for his forgiveness."

Hudson was touched by the sincerity in John R.'s voice. "I know you would, son, and I'm proud of you for wanting to. It's just that Mr. Edwards has to work some things out for himself. Why not give it some time. I'll probably be seeing him as this project unfolds. If the time is right, I'll give you the signal."

"Looks like I've got some of that—what did you call it?—unfinished business of my own now."

Hudson shook his head. "I'll help you all I can. If it's any consolation, I think I've completed the cycle on my own unfinished business."

"You're not going to ride through the Rockies on a motorcycle?"

"To tell the truth I had a hard time making it around a parking lot."

"There was some other stuff though too, wasn't there?" John R. inquired.

"Yes, but not worth talking about. I think I found out that I was after a life that was free of responsibilities and cares. It's pretty easy to imagine such an existence, but there is nowhere on earth that such a place exists. It's a daily grind, and there's no escaping it."

"It's possible to get help though," countered John R.

"Oh sure, you can pay a shrink to listen to your woes. In a rare instance or two some kind soul comes along to give you a helping hand. But mainly it's what I've known to be true all along—a person has to tough it out for himself, by himself. Every once in a while you get a lucky break. Preparation and opportunity meet each other in a dark alley, and you're back in business again."

"Is that what you think happened with this video project?" John R. asked.

"Can't be explained any other way, can it?"

"I believe it can." John R. spoke with a firmness and conviction which drew his father's attention. "Remember I told you about trusting Christ with my life?"

"Oh, that stuff," Hudson interrupted.

"Wait a minute," John R. argued. "It's not just 'that stuff.' I'm talking about some real substance. Ever since this necklace incident has taken place I've been nothing but confused. The preacher told me about prayer and . . ."

"Are you going to tell me that you prayed that the necklace was a phony, that Edwards was a Jew who was trying to stay hidden, and that I would get a chance to produce the video project?"

"No. Not even close. I asked for forgiveness for what I had done, and I asked for God's guidance in my life. I also asked for a way that the trouble between us could be healed."

Hudson was too moved by John R.'s last statement to make a wisecrack about it. "Why is this religious approach so important to you all of a sudden?"

"It's just a need I've got, Dad. I've got to be able to put my faith in something, and ever since I've put it in God, life has had some meaning for me."

"Can't you just believe in yourself a little more?"

"After what I did this summer? No . . . I need a little more than believing in myself. Y' know, I've been pretty critical of you. But when it came my turn to make decisions and do something on my own, I invented ways to blow it big-time."

Hudson was feeling uncomfortably warm in the quarters of the galley and asked that they go topside to the cockpit of the boat. "John R., I'm not being critical of your decision. I'm just trying to understand it. Look at that . . ." Hudson pointed up to the moon, which was shining full and brightly. "Men have walked up there. It's tough for me to believe that we're not capable of doing anything we set our minds to."

"But there was the *Challenger* disaster too, Dad. We're just as capable of lousing it up. I've been doing a lot of thinking lately. I've been seeing what man has done and what God has done, and they're not even in the same league."

"Such as?"

"Such as your situation with the stock market. It fell 500 points in one day, and you couldn't even get a call through to cut your losses. In the meantime there were all kinds of guys on the inside making a killing. Just when there's a new politician on the scene to save America, we learn that he is either fooling around with some bimbo or copying term papers in college. In my short career as a college student I can tell you that either of those charges was enough to get a person tossed out of school."

"What about the TV evangelists?"

"Same scenario, different players. We're so eager, so starved for leadership that we make stars out of anybody who sounds like they really believe in something. The preachers became the worshiped instead of the leaders of worship. People—that is, I just need to believe there is some order to this world."

"I guess it's fine if it works for you. I just can't see it myself," Hudson answered.

"Can't see it? Holy smokes, Dad, look around. We're surrounded by it. Did you see that deer tonight? She wasn't put together at some General Motors assembly plant. Look at this bay. You say how you love it. This is not a creation of Disney World. And you're getting a chance at a project which looked like it was in the tank only a month ago."

"It just seems so unbelievable."

"For you maybe, but not for me," John R. said with a touch of sadness.

"That's why you're going back to college? You've decided to be a preacher."

"Yes and no," John R. confessed. "I still don't have a clue

what I want to do, but now I'm convinced that God will show me the direction He wants me to take. I don't see myself as a preacher. I don't have that much to say."

Hoping to change the subject, Hudson looked at his watch. "It's nearly 1 o'clock," he said. "We'd better head back. How about staying at the house with me tonight?"

"Sounds good," said John R. "It's starting to get a little cold these nights. Fall is definitely coming on."

"I've got something I want to tell you," said Hudson.

"Yes?"

"Next week there will be a man here from Wisconsin to take the boat with him."

"What?" said John R. "You've sold *Angel Eyes?*"

"I'm afraid I had to. There was no action on the house up here, and I was getting short of funds. If I had known about the video deal a month ago, I may have been able to hold off, but . . ."

"Ah well . . . She's been a good boat, but there's a part of me that won't be sorry to see her go."

"Me too," thought Hudson.

"Dad, I've got something I want to tell you too. Remember when we were out here the last time and you told me how you were bothered because you never told your father that you loved him?"

"I remember," Hudson said softly.

"Well, I think you ought to hear it from me. I love you, Dad."

Two men over six feet tall stood on the back of a thirty-six-foot boat hugging each other. The older of the two clutched the younger tightly so he could hide the tears which were rolling down his cheeks.

In the distance, a fisherman let out a shout of joy.

THIRTY-SEVEN

J ohn R. reviewed the checklist one last time to make sure he had done every chore needed to close down the summer home. When he was certain that he had done everything satisfactorily, he lifted the duffel bag onto his shoulder and made his way toward the marina to meet the crew from Wisconsin who would be taking *Angel Eyes* across Lake Michigan to her new home. The cut trees which lined the street had been hauled away, and the village had begun work on paving the street, although it was obvious they could not complete the job before the winter snows would fall. What had once been a tree-lined gravel road was now a road of packed dirt barren of trees or shrubs. The wind swirled little tornadoes of dust around him as he walked. Several times he was forced to put down the duffel bag to wipe dust from his eyes. He was relieved when he made the paved streets in the village, even though they led him to the marina and the departure of the boat he had come to love the past five years.

The Wisconsin crew was from a brokerage house and knew the operating procedures of the Tiara very well. They offered to buy John R. lunch, but he declined saying he had a bus to catch. His last stop was at the Post Office to close the box which had been opened to receive mail. To his surprise there was another letter from his mother. He had just talked with her the prior evening to confirm the arrangements of his arrival.

He read the letter before he boarded the bus and three more times as he made his way toward home. It said,

Dear John R.,

As you know, your father and I are talking to each other again. I suppose it would be more accurate to say we are listening to each other again. I don't know what you said to your dad to get his attention, but he is much more attentive to what I say, and he says you deserve the credit.

You know how thrilled I am with your decision to go back to college, but it can't compare with the thrill you have given me by turning your life over to Christ. It would be a misstatement to say that your father is in complete agreement with our beliefs, but we must pray for him and love him, especially as he begins this new project. I don't know how the Lord is going to work this out, but I know that He will. I came across these verses from Isaiah 55:6-9 which assure us of it.

> *Seek the Lord while He may be found;*
> >   *call upon Him while He is near.*
> *Let the wicked forsake his way*
> >   *and the unrighteous man his thoughts;*
> *And let him return to the Lord,*
> >   *And He will have compassion on him;*
> *And to our God,*
> >   *"For My thoughts are not your thoughts,*
> *Neither are your ways My ways," declares the Lord.*
> >   *For as the heavens are higher than the earth,*
> *So are My ways higher than your ways*
> *And My thoughts than your thoughts.*

I can hardly wait to wrap my arms around you once again. I hope you have outgrown your self-consciousness about that. Even John Wayne kissed the girl once in a while—when his horse wasn't around.

Love,

Mom

He folded the letter and put it into his shirt pocket as the bus rolled to a stop in the terminal. As he came down the aisle toward the steps at the front of the bus, the driver stopped him. "Excuse me," said the driver, "but didn't I take you up to Westport about three or four months ago?"

"Yes, that's possible," answered John R. "Why do you ask?"

"Oh, I don't know. You just seem like a different kid to me than the one I took up there."

"I am." John R. smiled.

"Nothin' like a nice peaceful summer in the north country to help a fella relax, is there?"

"Almost nothing," John R. said as he stepped down from the bus. "Almost nothing at all."